I0666938

BOUND TO
ENDURE

~

JANEAL FALOR

BOUND TO ENDURE
Janeal Falor

© 2016 Janeal Falor
All Rights Reserved

ISBN-10: 0-9897432-8-4
ISBN-13: 978-0-9897432-8-0

To learn more about this author, please visit: www.janealfalor.com

Cover Photo by Damonza
www.damonza.com

Print Interior by Write Dream Repeat Book Design LLC
www.wdrbookdesign.com

First Edition
10 9 8 7 6 5 4 3 2 1

books in the
ELVEN PRINCESS SERIES

Bound by Birthright
Bound to Endure
Bound by Love

OTHER BOOKS BY JANEAL FALOR

MINE SERIES
Mine to Tarnish (Mine Prequel)
You Are Mine (Mine #1)
Mine to Spell (Mine #2)
Mine to Fear (Mine #3)
Sacrifice of Mine (Mine #4)

DARKENING LIGHT
Ever Darkening (Darkening Light #1)
Savage Light (Darkening Light #2)

For Karen
Thank you for always believing I can write

Chapter
ONE

❧

THE END OF THE AISLE arrives too quickly, but peace settles through me. Robert approved of this. Prince Phillip and I will end the conflict between elves and humans.

Constance and Jocelyn both move to lift the veil. I follow it with my gaze, looking at the prince's well-tailored clothes up to his broad shoulders.

With a pounding heart, I look into a face that's familiar. "Abner?"

"I'm sorry about everything," he says, expression contrite, his face is puckered like he doesn't want to be saying them.

How can this be? Why would he be here, an elf-hating human such as him. "What are you doing here?"

"I'm Prince Phillip. There'll be time to talk later, but I—"

"Wait, there won't be time to talk later because we'll be married. Everything will be said and done by then. You better explain yourself now."

He darts his gaze to the ground before meeting mine again. "The most important thing for you to know is that I lied."

"Of course you lied." I keep my voice down, despite wanting to yell. "That much is obvious. What exactly are you getting at?"

"Don't you see him? He's standing behind me."

I lift my gaze, and my chest lifts with it. Can it really be? Is he alive? He survived? And then I see him. Robert, his golden eyes watching me. He's alive.

And I'm about to marry his best friend.

"How can this be?" I try to sound stern when the only thing I feel is immense relief. All the pain and torment I felt over his death is thrust into uncertainty.

"Robert had nothing to do with it," Abner says. Or rather it's Prince Phillip now. This is so confusing. "He woke up soon after we left you on Captain Smythe's ship, said we needed to go back, but I refused. By the time we returned to my parents, he had everyone convinced we needed to put the betrothal back on. Everyone except me.

"When my parents heard his reasoning—that our two people needed to unite and that you would be a good match— they agreed with Robert. After they dictated their reply to your call, I had the scribe sneak in a few lines."

"No." Those few lines were news on Robert's death. Pain rakes through me. All this time I thought Robert was dead, and it was a lie from my future husband?

"I'm afraid it's true. I was bitter that I had to marry an elf." He sounds as if he's still bitter but resigned. "Bitter that the elf is in love with my best friend. So I had the scribe write that

Robert died. You see, I am the prince. Abner is my middle name. People do as I command."

I don't care if he's the prince of not; I want to spit on him like he spat on me. "That was cruel. If it weren't for our two races needing this, I would leave right now." I keep my voice low but dangerous.

He frowns. "You have every right to."

And I should. He deserves to be left, not permanently attached to me. It's not fair that I have to stay. Not fair that I have to marry him. But how can I leave? How can I let my people down like that?

"I won't go." My voice sounds as dejected as I feel. At least Robert is alive, and looking on with an expression that's hard to read. It's more than I hoped for. More than I thought possible—but not nearly enough. "We can't start our marriage on lies," I say.

"That's why I'm coming forward with the whole truth. As much as I wish it wasn't so, both our countries need this."

And what about me? I almost ask, but I can't bring myself to. He clearly doesn't care; I'm lucky he cares about my country enough to marry me despite that. Though I suppose I have Robert to thank for that.

Robert.

I give him another glance. His broad shoulders look exactly like what I need to cry on this moment, but that will never happen. I take in the rest of his features, his brown eyes and sandy hair. Everything about him screams at me to run to him, to find myself in his arms, but there's a whole crowd of people as a reason why I can't.

What will it be like, being married to the best friend of the man I love—a best friend who's shown little kindness to my people? Well, except that time he tried to fight back when pirates tied up Emeline and Robert. That's the only hint of kindness I've seen from him. What will he be like as a husband? Even if Robert says he's a good guy, I can't believe it.

The priest clears his throat. "May I begin?"

Please, no. I look at Robert. His golden eyes are brimming with sadness, but he nods, as if saying he understands. I can't believe I'm about to marry a man I hate while the man who may be my true love stands a few feet from us, alive and well.

"Proceed." This time I use a formal voice. In control. Much better than the torrent of anger and heartbreak swirling inside me. I turn to Abner. "But you have a lot to make up for."

He clenches his teeth, but nods.

The crowd is making all sorts of noise. I don't know if they heard what we said—I hope not—but they clearly know something is amiss. My massive, diamond-covered wedding gown hinders my moving around easily so I can't run away. Maybe it's overcompensating for my ugly looks, but I wish it was a normal gown. Something simple. But if I don't like my groom, I may as well not like my dress.

Abner nods at the officiator. The man mumbles something in reply, but I ignore him. The only thing I need to do is agree to this inane marriage, and then I'm out of here. Jocelyn stands close by, her eyes wide. Constance has a knowing, sorrowful gaze about her. I want to go sob to them both, but that would cause more talk than I've already done. None of this is fair.

My parents and the human king and queen are watching the scene with eager gazes, like they want us to get a move on and make this happen. I look to my mother, hoping she'll give me some sign. Some leeway. A few minutes to breathe. But she holds her head higher when I look at her, reminding me to do the same. It's my place to be elegant, no matter the circumstances.

I glance at Robert. He runs a hand through his hair, and it's like a dagger to my chest. I forgot how much I like that gesture. How much I enjoyed his hand holding mine.

I turn away from these useless thoughts and stare past the officiator into the forest. The priest begins, droning on about who knows what. I can't stand listening. The forest is calm, if nothing else is. A way to get calm is exactly what I need right now, and though the forest helps, it's not nearly enough.

The crowd never settles back down, and there's a low hum coming from them. They're as restless as I am, though I doubt they're as conflicted.

Was that a flash of something behind them? Next to me, Abner tenses, and I respond likewise. What's going on? I see nothing more, but I hear the clang of swords hitting one another. Then screams.

As I look farther past the audience, the confusion morphs into a blow of panic at the sight of Captain Smythe's massive frame, surrounded by his dirty crew.

Chapter

TWO

❧

FEAR SHOOTS ICY FINGERS through my body, planting me to the spot. The world sways around me. At first I think I'm fainting, but then I realize Robert has burst over and twirled me around so I'm shielded by him. A thrill goes through me at being so near him again, but now isn't the time to linger on such feelings.

The crowd turns to mass confusion, everyone bolting away from the charging pirates. Stewart appears out of nowhere and hands Abner and Robert a sword each.

"Where's mine?" I ask.

"Not today," Stewart says, brandishing his own sword.

"Take her," Robert says to Constance. "Keep her safe."

Before she can do so, I grab Robert's hand. I can't help it. Time seems to slow and stretch as we touch, and a trill of warmth calms me, starting where our hands touch and reaching outward. It's like a balm to the despair that's ached through me since I was told he died. He gives my hand a squeeze, and I know he feels it too. No matter what happens, we will always have a connection.

If anyone was going to get married, this should have been Robert and me—uniting elves and humans between a Princess and a… well, he can't be a common sailor if he's best friends with the prince. Who is he?

There's not time to think. He lets go, and Constance takes my other hand and yanks me in the opposite direction. I shake my head to clear my thoughts of anything but escape and the warmth of his hand on mine.

Despite wanting to fight, I run, forcing myself to keep up with Constance. She's my rock. If she can run fast, then so can I. I hear someone breathing close behind and find Jocelyn racing with us, a determined look on her face. Together, the three of us run over the grassy knoll, heading for the forest.

My foot catches on something. I fly to the ground and slam hard to the grass. My face and side ache where the diamonds crush into me. A funny thought hits me. I probably got a grass stain on my wedding dress. Mother will not approve.

I brush the thought away as Constance kneels at my side. "Are you all right?" she asks.

I nod, the only thing I can manage.

"Good. We have to keep going." She helps me to my feet.

She's right; the fight is already getting closer. The clanging, clashing, and yelling grows louder. Abner, Stewart, and Robert are holding the line with my guards in the back nearest us. As much as I wish to join the fight, I have to get out of here. My presence would be more of a distraction than a help.

We dart through the forest. When did we get so close to it? My lungs burn, and my legs ache. Though I've been working harder to keep myself in better condition since my long trek home from Sulamay Island and the threat of Captain Smythe there, it hasn't included running this hard with a burdensome gown on. My breathing becomes desperate as I slow. Without a word, we come to a stop, hidden within the woods.

I bend in half the best I can and try to catch my breath. When it slows, I straighten back up. Worry pierces through me, and I twist my hand among the diamonds on my dress, feeling their cold uselessness.

"I have to go back to them." Back to him.

Constance puts a hand on my shoulder. "No. You need to stay here. They'll be fine, but we need to keep you safe."

Which I know in my head, but my heart is saying the forest is the wrong place to be. I need to be back on the field. Need to make certain my parents are well. That the human king and queen are fine. That my people are safe. That no one is getting hurt.

That Robert isn't getting hurt.

"What if something happens to them?" I ask.

Jocelyn scoots closer and wraps an arm around me. That action alone calms me more than words. The girl who's become a sister to me knows better than anyone else how much I'm hurting. How this has been too much for me to know what to do with.

"They'll be fine," Constance says. "After the last fight, Captain Smythe was left with few men. It looks like he may have gained a few since, but not many. Not enough to beat our guard." She leans closer to whisper, "Robert will be fine."

I squeeze my eyes shut and try to believe the words Constance spoke. The ones she was brave enough to say, that I shouldn't be pining after a man I'm not to marry. I've seen Robert fight before, and he's more than capable of handling himself. He's strong and sure.

Only, he left that fight unconscious. Who knows if he would have made it without me there to heal him, and this time I'm not close by.

I'm needed.

Jocelyn lets out a sharp gasp and tightens her grip around me. I let my eyelids fly open, and I let out my own shocked gasp.

Captain Smythe chortles, his massive hands at his waist. "Hello, Princess. I see this time I have you within my clutches. They'll be no escaping. Aiden, take the princess."

Someone shifts beside Captain Smythe, and I take in those surrounding him. Despair claws at me as I see the large number of pirates. More than I remember being on the ship last time he was in Amara to kidnap me with Octavian's help.

One of the pirates stands out among the rest—the one who moves, who I assume is Aiden. But he can't possibly be with the pirates. There's no way. Even after Octavian and Captain Smythe getting together, it doesn't seem right. He's not a human at all, but an elf. What's he doing with a group of humans, and not just any group, but pirates?

Aiden's white hair is down to his shoulders, rare for a male of my kind, and moves in the slight breeze building up. Though his hair is white, his face is youthful, as if he's only a handful of years older than I am. His cheek bones stand out, emphasizing his pale green eyes. He steps closer to me, making me realize I'm gaping. I harden my expression and try to devise a way out of this mess.

"Don't you dare touch her," Constance hisses.

"Go ahead, Aiden," Captain Smythe's baritone rumbles. "I warn you not to stand in my way today, old one."

Before I know what happens, Aiden grabs me and flitters me into the midst of the pirates. The stench of body odor makes me gag. They're rough and filthy and about to be my captors. There has to be a spell I can cast to stop this.

"*No.*" Jocelyn's high-pitched voice is frantic. "You can't take her."

"George, grab the human girl," Captain Smythe says, ignoring her. "I believe we can find a use for her. Let's get out of here."

I kick Aiden in the shin, but he ignores me. I proceed to struggle as one of the pirates steps toward Jocelyn while the rest of them move forward toward the sea. Constance tries to come to us, but one of the pirates hits her to the ground.

Aiden yanks me away like I weigh nothing, but I continue fighting as best I can. There's a shuffle of movement from the direction we just left, but it's drowned in Jocelyn's kicks and squeals.

"Don't you dare touch me with your dirty hands. Stop it right now."

"'Nough of that, wench." The pirate's bellow is followed by the smack of skin hitting skin.

I wince and cry out, "Leave her alone."

I try to look over at Jocelyn. Aiden pushes me so hard I almost fall, until he grabs me by the wrist. He locks both of my arms behind me, his grasp digging into me as we leave the forest. What can I do to stop them? Magic doesn't seem enough against so many.

Still I have to try. I try to bend over to reach for the ground to make a root for them to trip over, but Aiden jerks me to a standing position.

My feet slop over the sandy beach, making it harder to remain upright. Aiden tightens his grip so hard I cry out in pain, and then he lets go. I fall to the sand, and my nose and mouth fill with the stuff. I lift my head and spit out all I can, trying not to curse.

"You will not take her," Constance's voice rings out.

I jerk my head up to find her with a large stick in one hand. Aiden is pulling himself up from the ground, blood seeping down his head. The sound of a sword being drawn from its scabbard sends a wave of panic through me. Struggling to get up, I try to reach Constance. She's coming closer and closer, that hard steel of hers showing with each movement. If I can touch her, maybe I can clear my head enough to help us escape.

Without a word, Captain Smythe steps toward Constance and slashes his sword straight through her midsection. She drops to the ground, the deep wound already creating a dark pull of crimson liquid beside her.

"No." As I continue toward her, tears stream down my cheeks. I can't make sense of what's before me.

Jocelyn's shrill cry is incoherent. The pirate that holds her clamps his hand over her mouth, muffling the sound. I stumble, right myself, and race toward Constance.

"Don't let her touch the old one," Captain Smythe barks.

Several hands clamp on me, halting my progress. Rage fills me with a white-hot light. Tingling magic courses through me until it reaches every inch of my skin. Its power is stronger than any I've ever felt before, consumed with my need to get to Constance. Not worrying about the consequences, I let it surge outward. The hands holding me withdraw, and cries of pain fill the air.

Tears blur my vision as I bend over Constance. My heart aches so fiercely, it's like it received a pierce from a sword of its own. Constance's eyes flutter but don't open. I lunge down and move to touch her face.

Aiden clamps his hand around my wrist.

"No. I have to heal her." The words come out in a fearful shriek.

I reach for my magic again and feel the sensation stir within my chest. Suddenly, it's gone. I call for it again, desperate, but the familiar tingling won't come.

"What's going on?" I ask. "This can't be happening. I have to save her."

Aiden snorts and pulls me away from Constance, who grows paler. "Don't like losing out on your magic, huh? Too bad it left at such an inconvenient time."

I snap to attention, not at his words, but at the power emanating from him. "What are you doing to me? You have to stop. Let me save her, and I will come with you willingly."

"What do you think, Captain? Should we grant her request?" Aiden smirks.

"Please," I say. "*Please.*" I glance at Constance. Terror plunges through me at the sight of her slowing breathing.

"I'll do anything you want. You have to let me save her. She's going to die without my help."

As I talk, I try to pull away from him, to get my magic back and get closer to Constance. They can't just leave her here. They can't.

Captain Smythe rubs his jaw with one of his massive hands and chuckles. "Nah. I've taken more insult from that hag then I've ever taken from anyone else. She deserves it. Besides, with Aiden on my side, you have no recourse but to do what I want."

I slump, all hope crashing out of me. Aiden catches me before I hit the ground. I can't bring myself to care. Over the laughter of the group of pirates, there's the sound of Jocelyn sobbing. My face is wet as I look at Constance. The edges of my vision blacken as I wait for her chest to move. My body is numb with despair at its stillness. As Aiden drags me toward the water, blackness closes in and steals me away.

Chapter
THREE

~

MY HEAD FEELS AS IF someone is trying to squeeze it into a tight ball. There's a distant moan. I attempt to wrench my eyes open, but they flutter, refusing to stay that way. Whatever I'm lying on is stiff against my back. A gentle rocking side to side adds to the sick feeling in my stomach.

I search through my memory, trying to find out where I am and what took place to get me here, but all I find is more pain. Why does it hurt so? Another moan sounds, this time closer. A wet trickle soothes my dry lips.

"Shh. It's all right," Jocelyn whispers in my ear. "I'm here, but please try and keep quiet. I don't want them to know you're awake until they have to."

Who's not supposed to know I'm awake? And why? The thoughts slice through my head and help clear things up some. Why would Jocelyn want to keep me quiet? I realize I'm moaning.

My head aches something fierce, and I'm remembering something... about Robert. *Robert.* I try to sit up at the thought of leaving him behind with the pirates, but Jocelyn holds me down.

"Robert?" I barely hear the raspy word coming from my lips.

She places her hand on my arm. Her silence increases my worry. The sway of my body reminds me of being on a boat. A ship? How did I get on a ship? The pirates. Captain Smythe. *Constance.*

I work to keep from calling out. Pain rips through my heart, shredding it, at the memory of Constance's still chest. It can't be. Not her. Anyone but her.

I force my eyes open. The room is dark. It takes a moment, but my sight adjusts. There are wooden walls around me and Jocelyn as far as I can see. The dimness makes it difficult. Jocelyn's eyes are swollen. She drips more water in my mouth, but I don't feel like drinking. I want to slap away the offering, curl up in a ball, and cry. But crying never helps in a situation like this one. Crying will have to come later.

Besides, my mouth is dry, and my stomach is aching. I swallow the pain away—both physically and emotionally — and ask, "Where are we?"

"Captain Smythe's ship. You've been unconscious for a week. I've been so worried about you. It's been hard giving you water. I'm so glad to finally see you awake and responding. Aiden told Captain Smythe you would awake, that it was a consequence of your spell—using up all that energy in one go to shock those around you. I've never seen anything like it." Her voice remains low. "I didn't believe him, though. I was so afraid you'd never wake up."

I think back to the power coursing through me. Aiden's assessment sounds about right. Other thoughts come—thoughts of one who's dear to me. I want to push them away for a time when I can properly deal with them, but I have to know. "It's all true, then. They took us in the woods and brought us here. Constance is…"

Jocelyn sniffs. "Yes."

Fresh tears start falling. Jocelyn wraps her arms around me, and we sob silently. The pain is absolute, worse than any I've ever known before, even when I thought Robert had died. My heart feels as if someone froze it and threw it on a rock to shatter it into a thousand pieces.

There's no healing from grief such as this.

We cry until the light drifting under the door of the room brightens. She hurries to pull away, her youthful cheeks glistening with the new light. Her normally full of life green eyes are red and dull. Seeing her like this tears at me even more.

A shuffling noise comes from outside the door.

"Act asleep," Jocelyn whispers.

Unsure why it's so important, I hurry to brush away the tears, close my eyes, and turn my head toward the wall. She's the only person I left that's trustworthy, and I know I can trust her with my life. She takes a seat.

The door creaks open, and two sets of footsteps trample in, one of which sends heavy vibrations through the bunk I'm on.

"Is she awake yet?" Aiden's voice makes me want to jump up and scream. If only he'd let me touch Constance, she might still be alive. I work to keep my body still and my breathing even.

"Not yet." Jocelyn's voice quivers.

"That's odd. I thought she'd be awake by now," he mutters.

"Are you sure she'll wake up? Perhaps you were wrong," Captain Smythe says.

The anger that poured through me before is nothing compared to the molten hot fury that pours through me now. Rage seeps in my bones. I want to draw my sword and slash it through him like he did to Constance. He killed her, and then he just left her there.

But I'm getting too worked up. I can't give myself away. It takes every amount of will power I can muster not to move and keep my breaths even.

"She will wake," Aiden says. "She has to. I wonder..."

One set of footsteps thuds closer to the bunk.

"Please don't disturb her," Jocelyn says. "Haven't you done enough damage yet?"

"Get out of the way."

The bunk shifts next to me as she moves off it. "You have us now. We aren't going anywhere. Just let her rest. She obviously needs it."

I'm surprised by the force of her words.

The sharp whack is followed by a body falling to the ground. I bolt upward, eyes open. My brain beats violently against my skull with the movement. Captain Smythe's colossal frame takes up most of the cabin. Standing in front of him, Aiden is smug. Jocelyn is crumpled on the floor under him. She looks up at me with concern in her eyes.

"Do not touch her. I'm what you want. Leave her alone." I struggle to get the words out. Each one is like a knife stabbing through my head. "Are you all right, Jocelyn?"

Her face is bunched with tension, but she nods. Captain Smythe pushes past Aiden and gives Jocelyn a swift kick in the stomach. She screams, and I grab him, trying to pull him away from her. He shrugs me off as if I weigh less than a strand of hair.

"Get used to it." His face widens with a wicked smile, and I shrink back. "That's right, Princess. We aren't playing so nice this time without Octavian to call the shots."

I look down so he doesn't see my face, rage and fear mingling in a dangerous combination I can't let out. "Please, I beg of you, do what you want with me but leave her alone."

He snorts. "Funny. That's what she's been saying all week about you. Guess that gives me free reign to do whatever I want to both of you."

He grips his arm around my back. With his other hand, he reaches up to my head. A hand as big as my head. Fear takes hold of me.

He yanks me up and bends closer to give me a once over. "Understand this, little Princess. I'll do whatever pleases me."

Aiden coughs. "Captain Smythe."

He releases me so abruptly I fly down to the bunk with a crash. "Yes?"

"She is awake and well, like I said she would be."

Narrowing his eyes at Aiden, Captain Smythe responds, "Luckily for you, she is."

Aiden stands straighter. "Is that a threat?"

"Of course not." Captain Smythe turns back to me. "My dear, Aiden will be keeping a very close eye on you. As you have already discovered, he can thwart any attempts you make at casting a spell, if needed. If you step out of line, I'll be sure to make Jocelyn pays for your actions." His soft, caring voice makes me squirm more than his threat. "And there will be a guard outside your door at all times."

He runs a finger along my jaw line and then gives my cheek a rough tap. Laughing, he leaves the room with Aiden trailing behind him. The door slams shut after the two of them are gone.

Last time, Captain Smythe clearly was holding back, as we guessed he was. Fear sinks through me, mellowing my rage. How are we ever going to survive this?

Chapter
FOUR

~

I STRUGGLE TO PULL MYSELF off the bunk, my wedding dress not only uncomfortable, but also matted and dirty. My hair feels about the same.

"Are you all right, Jocelyn? I'm so sorry," I say.

Clutching her arms around her midsection, she mumbles, "I'm fine."

"You're not." I try to sit on the wooden floor, next to her. It takes some maneuvering, but I manage it. "Here. Let me heal you."

She pulls away. "No. Please, my lady, don't waste your strength on me. Neither of us can afford to lose out on anything. We don't know how long they'll leave us alone for, and we may yet need our strength."

"I thought you'd finally gotten used to calling me Arabella." I sigh. "Just let me heal you. I'll be fine. I doubt they'll come back for a while." I hope.

"No." She shakes her head. "They've been doing this the whole time you were asleep. Sometimes they'd leave, only to turn around and come right back. Other times, they waited a long time. Once, more than a day."

The whole time I've been asleep? A sick knot forms in my stomach. How has she survived this type of neglect? I rub her back, hoping she won't notice the healing spell I'm casting. It's only a little one, because I don't want to completely go against her wishes, but she needs something.

She does have a point, though. How long are we going to be like this? Where are they taking us, and what plans do they have? I hate to think too hard on that. Between the rumors and knowing what happens around Captain Smythe, I know we may never make it out of here. I want to sob for a week. Instead, I force myself to stay strong.

I have to. Jocelyn needs me to. I need me to.

"They're playing games." I stand and help her up. She needs to get more comfortable, where her body can heal itself better.

She takes my hand and stands with a grimace. "Yes, well, I wish Constance was here, to let them have it."

I wince at the sound of her name. "Take a seat on the bunk."

"I'm fine."

She's clearly not fine. I get a good look at her for the first time and gasp. "What happened to your face?"

"It's nothing." She puts her hands over her cheeks. "I'm fine."

"But those bruises." They range from a sickly green to a dark purple. Almost her entire face is covered with them, and her lip is split open. Anger simmers below the surface, but I keep a tight lid on it. "Did Captain Smythe or one of his men do this?"

Her voice is faint. "Both."

I clench my fists. If only I had my sword, I'd show them a thing or two. "I wish I could release the spell I used on them before."

"After how long you were out, I'm not sure that's a good idea. I was so frightened for you. What was that spell anyway? I've never seen anything like it. Watching those pirates jump away from you in agonizing pain sure was gratifying, though."

I give a small smile. I sit on the bunk, hoping my action will convince her to sit as well. Thankfully, when I motion for her to do so, she does. "I'm not sure," I say. "I've never felt such power. It was like a concentration of energy built up inside and then burst out through every part of me. I felt the energy, but it didn't hurt me."

"That's amazing. I admit I don't know much about magic, but I think I'd have heard if someone did something like that previously."

"It's not something I've heard of either." And the power of it scares me a little. "I don't know where it came from. I wonder if I could harness it again. I wasn't paying attention to my actions. I was trying to get to Constance."

Saying her name brings back a fresh wave of pain, stark and unrelenting. I can't believe she's gone. How will I ever survive without her? I need her. She's more a mother to me than my own mother is. Who will guide me through things? Who will scold me when I do something wrong? I need that look she gives me, the one that puts me back to the path I should be on.

"I can't believe it really happened," Jocelyn says. "The whole time you were asleep, the scene replayed in my head. I knew Captain Smythe was a brutal man, but after the way he treated us before… I don't know. I guess I thought the rumors weren't true—that maybe he wasn't all that bad, and it was just a bunch of talk."

"That's what I thought, too. I wonder what was holding him back before? He wasn't exactly kind to us before, but I didn't expect this of him. I'd give anything to have it all be a bad dream." Tears swim in my eyes. Whether I want them there or not, they need to come.

"This is worse than any nightmare." She shivers. "Why do you think he took us? I doubt he came for me. He only grabbed me because I happened to be there. But with Octavian banished, I thought this would all be over."

I brush the tears off my cheeks and force myself to focus on her question. "I'm not sure. I hadn't thought of it yet."

"I've had too much time to think."

I curse myself for not waking sooner. Stupid spell consequence. "Depending on where he's taking us, I may end up with too much time as well. Speaking of time, I'm hungry and need to take care of some private business. Have they made accommodations for such?"

She wrinkles her nose and points to a bucket in the corner of the room. "They've been emptying that once a day. As for food, it's been sporadic. I saved a little, though."

After I take care of business, she opens the top drawer of a small dresser near the dark corner of the room and pulls out a biscuit. "Sorry there isn't more. There's some water if you need it. They didn't leave us with enough."

"Thank you." I take the proffered biscuit, split it in half, and offer one part to her.

"No. You go ahead and eat it. I've been eating most of what they brought for the last few days, though it wasn't much. You've only had the water I managed to give you."

"Are you certain? It doesn't sound like they've been feeding you enough, and I'll have a hard time eating even this much anyway. You know how boats make my stomach queasy."

She looks at me warily, the bruises on her face breaking my heart. "Are you sure? Because I can last until they bring more."

"Please." I shove half the biscuit in her hand, though I could eat it and still be hungry, and nibble on my own. There's another bucket on the dresser with a cup and a damp rag beside it. "Is that clean water?" I ask.

She nods, her mouth full with the portion of the biscuit I gave her. I reach up, dip the cup into the bucket of water and fill it. I bring it to my mouth and take a tentative sip. The water is warm and stale. I drink the entire cup and then refill it and hand it to Jocelyn before I finish my dry biscuit. The light coming in from the door is fading, highlighting the mis-shapen planks of the floor.

"Do you think they'll come back soon?" I ask.

She shrugs. "I don't know. They never seem to come when I expect it. Sometimes Aiden comes alone. He creeps me out as much as Captain Smythe does."

"Why would he be with Captain Smythe?" It's very unusual for an elf to take up with humans. Though after the last few months—what with Octavian conspiring with Captain Smythe—maybe it's not as uncommon as I thought.

"I don't know." She sighs. "There are too many things I don't have an answer for. I'm sorry."

"It's fine. I don't expect you to have all the answers, especially in circumstances such as these. Maybe we get some sleep while we can. I know I've been sleeping a lot, but I still feel tired." A yawn escapes me, proving my point. "You take the bunk tonight. I'll sleep on the floor."

"You can't. It's not fitting for a princess."

I let out a small giggle. "I can too, silly. I'm quite capable of it. Besides, I assume I've been on the bunk the whole time. It's your turn to get a decent night's sleep. Or at least as good as you can here. If it was bigger, I'd share with you, but as is, there's barely enough room for one."

"But—"

"I insist." I slide to the floor and wince when I hear a mouse scamper under the bunk. Good thing she can't see my face. The last thing I want to do is sleep down here with the mice. Gross. "Try to get some sleep."

She lies down and curls up in a ball. "Thank you."

"You're welcome."

I stretch my frame out. The night won't be a restful one, but hopefully I'll be able to maintain my energy. What lies in store for us? Where is Captain Smythe even taking us? What is he going to do with us once we get there?

And where is Robert? Losing Constance is too much on its own; I can't imagine losing him again.

I can't bear to watch them treat Jocelyn this way. I'm afraid of how I may react. Whatever I do will be repaid in kind, probably worse than anything I dole out. How are we ever going to survive this?

Chapter
FIVE

∾

JOCELYN AND I ALTERNATE between sleeping, talking, and meditating for what seems to be about two days. It's difficult to discern in this dark bunk, but the light comes and disappears twice. Captain Smythe and Aiden stay away, which gives me some peace but no food or water. If they come around, I'm not sure what I'll do, but it wouldn't be good.

"Your face is looking better," I tell Jocelyn. "Does it hurt very much?"

"Just a little now," she replies. "Do you think they're coming with food soon?"

My stomach rumbles. Apparently caring about me being awake and being fed are two very different concerns. I've never gone so long without food in my entire life. The ache of hunger is one I've never known before. "I don't know."

Silence returns as it always does. How much is there to talk about when you're locked aboard a pirate ship, scared for your life and having lost someone you love deeply? "I miss Constance. She'd know what to do now, even if it would just be muttering about our poor treatment."

"Yeah." Jocelyn gives a little laugh. "More likely she'd be banging on the door, demanding food. Once they gave her what they think is food, she'd be demanding to work in the kitchen. She'd figure out a way to make it in there, too. Then she'd have them bowing and scraping to her because of how good her meals are."

I laugh. "That sounds about right."

In the lull that follows, I think more on her, at least the little she let me know about her. Her true love, whom she left in order to care for me. Andries. She was in contact with him again, if only to have the scroll we found restored.

Does he know of her death yet? Who will tell him? Who is there, besides me and my mother, who knows how much they meant to each other? Mother certainly won't bring herself to say anything. She probably doesn't know they were in contact again. Appearances mean so much to her.

What must she and my father be thinking right now? Are they looking for me? Do they know Captain Smythe took me? I can't imagine how frantic they must be. Last month, when I came home after they thought I'd been kidnapped, they were more a mess than I'd ever seen them. This is even worse; I'm not presumed dead. They must know Captain Smythe has me after his attack, and that alone is reason to fret.

The door opens, and I flinch away from the light.

A pirate plops a plate of food and a bucket of water on the dresser. "Bucket," he says, referring to the one we've been using for our necessities.

Jocelyn runs to get the soiled bucket from the corner and gives it to him. He swaps it out for a new one and slams the door closed.

"Guess that's all we get for now," I say, thankful it wasn't someone to torture Jocelyn or me.

"It's enough. That bucket smelled," she says. "We'd better ration the food, in case it's a while before they come back."

I glance at the plate. Two slices of salted pork and four biscuits. That's not nearly enough food after as long as we've been waiting. "It's a good thing you're here, or I'd be making some really bad choices." I pause a moment, my words catching up with me. "Actually, as grateful as I am for your presence, I wish you didn't have to be here."

"Neither of us should be."

WHAT SEEMS LIKE WEEKS but is only a few days later, Aiden opens the door to our prison. A cold chill wraps around my chest.

"Let's go." He grabs me by the wrist and yanks me through the door. "Don't try anything."

I stumble, my legs not accustomed to the quick movements after I've been locked up this long. Behind me, I hear Jocelyn scrambling to catch up. The moon, half covered by clouds, lights the way across the deck. A few pirates watch our procession toward one side of the deck, but the ship is mostly empty.

A pirate with rippling muscles is waiting at the railing. He yanks me from Aiden and tosses me up in his arms, his foul body odor overwhelming me.

"Put me down," I say, trying to create as much distance from him as I can.

The pirate laughs. I wish I was in a position to kick him.

"Remember I'm not far." Aiden narrows his eyes at me and then swings himself over the railing. Seconds later, he calls up from below. "Ready."

Ready for what? Before I can form another thought, the burly pirate heaves me over the railing and flings me out of his arms. My scream fills the silent night air as I plummet toward the ocean. I tense with my back to the water, preparing to hit the sea.

Strong arms catch me around the knees and shoulders, and the boat rocks violently with the impact. No water, then. They tossed me over the side into a waiting boat. Aiden sits down and shoves me to the side. He clamps one arm around my waist, making movement near impossible.

I want him off of me. "What? Don't you trust me?"

He ignores me, turning to watch Jocelyn make her descent down the rope ladder. They could have let me climb down like her. Am I really that much of a threat? Maybe it's a good thing to be perceived as such. If only there was more I could do about it if I weren't afraid of the consequences that would befall Jocelyn.

Taking a seat next to me, Jocelyn gives me a relieved smile. The pirate who threw me jumps in after her and takes his place at the head of the boat. The squished vessel tilts toward the heavy man and starts forward of its own accord.

Jocelyn gasps. "How does it do that?"

Turning to her with a smirk, Aiden says, "Magic. I change the waves under the boat in such a way that it goes where I want."

I notice his hand in the water outside the boat, the moonlight shining down on it. I hope a fish bites him. "Most elves aren't like you," I say. "I can't understand why you use magic so much. You really shouldn't be so careless with it. There is a price to be paid."

"Nothing important," he says. This will only cause the boat to wear out faster. Captain Smythe has more than enough supplies."

I shiver in the night air, but not from the temperature. I look around, ignoring Aiden's glare. It's difficult to distinguish much of the landscape in the night. A black mountain looms over us. Though I can't see any signs of a dock, there must be one, because we're headed straight for the mountain.

I glance at Jocelyn and try to give her a comforting smile. She quivers. I wish Aiden wasn't holding me down so I could go over to her and comfort her. Salty sea air fills my nose. I take a deep breath, welcoming the change from the dank cabin we were stuck in for too long.

We're closer to the dark mass now. The sound of waves lapping against the land grows louder. The dark mound ahead of us fills the sky. It makes me nervous how close we're getting to it without signs of slowing. Soon, it devours everything—stars and all. Though I can't see, I can feel the presence of a cave's roof and hear the echoes off a distant wall. How do they know where they're going in the absolute darkness?

A faint light ahead catches my attention. It flickers but grows as we move toward it. Soon, I'm able to make out the dim outline of the pirate and Aiden. I shift my gaze to Jocelyn. Her face is still bruised but clearing up. Her eyes wise to what's going on, never leaving the light.

I turn back toward the light and notice a small entrance about the size of a door. The hole looks like it's been carved out of the rock. Music and voices drift to us. It sounds as if someone is having a party. Not the sort of noise I expected around Captain Smythe.

The boat stops on red stone next to the fire. After jumping out of the boat, the pirate ties it next to several others. What do they have going on down here? I suppose I'm about to find out.

Aiden removes his arm from around my waist. I head toward Jocelyn, but he snatches my wrist and wrenches me out of the boat. I trip after him, barely keeping myself from landing face first on the rock. As we head toward the door-way-like opening, my heart is pounding.

We move through the doorway, and I blink to adjust to the sudden brightness. The cavern we stand in is enormous. A bonfire roars in the center of the room, but several smaller fires are scattered around the edge, giving a smoky scent to the air. If Aiden wasn't dragging me along, I would have stopped in shock at the number of people inside.

There are probably about one hundred people here, not all of whom look like pirates. I've never seen a female accompanying Captain Smythe, but here there are more of them than males. Their shadows dance across the red rock walls.

Aiden shoves his way through the crowd, pulling me with him. I glance back to find the pirate who accompanied us on the boat prodding Jocelyn forward. She gives me a small smile, probably to let me know she sees me and is being brave.

From somewhere in the room, the music switches to a new song. Drums beat in time to the swaying dancers. The speech around me is slurred, and the cave stinks of not just smoke but alcohol. At least that's one thing in our favor. A drunk captor will be easier to escape.

Aiden thrusts me forward so abruptly I fly to the ground. My knees scream in pain as they connect with the rock. Jocelyn lands beside me but catches herself. She grunts as her skin slaps against the stone.

A large hand grabs my head and turns my view away from Jocelyn to face forward. Dark pants are all I see until the hand jerks my head up. Captain Smythe hulks overs me with a sadistic grin on his face. The music and chatter ceases.

"Finally here, I see." His speech is clear. It's just as well; maybe he's a mean drunk.

He grabs me by the hair and yanks. Pain shrieks on my scalp, and I struggle to stand to take the pressure off. I lock my jaw, trying not to scream. He motions for Jocelyn to get up, and she leaps to her feet, shaking under his gaze.

"Men, take a look at my prize." Captain Smythe's voice reverberates across the room.

Murmurs of approval sweep the cavern. He finally unclenches his hand, and I give myself a moment to relax, to ease from the pain, though my head is still throbbing. My reprieve is short-lived. He wraps his arm around my shoulder, making all of the tension fly back. He reaches out and grabs Jocelyn to his other side.

The crowd only has a few dirty bodies, the rest of the people are surprisingly clean. Their ages vary. Though there are no children here, I do spot a woman thick with child. Each gaze I meet seems hungrier than the last. I cringe. I don't want to know what they hope to gain from me. I lower my head.

It takes a concentrated effort to hold myself together. To not react. There's nothing I can do against him in a room full of Captain Smythe's comrades and what appears to be his followers. The only things I can do would lead to more trouble. I have to hold on for now. I have to last.

"Does anyone feel like playing?" Captain Smythe asks. Cheers go up all around, and he chuckles. "Have at this one."

He propels Jocelyn into the crowd of grabbing hands. I dive after her, but the captain tightens his hold on me, pulling me back. He swings me up in the air and sits in a chair, making me end up in his lap. I want to vomit down the front of him. Instead, when he does nothing threatening, I search the crowd for Jocelyn. She sits in a chair, a group surrounding her.

A woman spits in Jocelyn's face. "Elf lover."

"No. Leave her alone," I yell, but Aiden is the only one to turn toward her, anger flaming in his eyes. The question is: anger at Jocelyn or at the woman?

Captain Smythe forces me to look at him. "This is my empire. My comrades, who no one knows about. What do you think of it?"

I glance over the room, taking it in with new eyes. No wonder he can get away with doing so much damage; he has a lot of people supporting and helping him. "I think it's rather small, compared to my kingdom," I say.

"Your kingdom is nothing but a bunch of wimpy ninnies."

I tense at the words, wanting to slap him across the face. My people are anything but wimps. But now isn't the time to fight it.

In a voice only I can hear, he asks, "Where's Octavian?"

What? This is the last thing I expected. "I don't know. Crimson Ruins, I guess."

"He's not there. Try again."

How can he not be there? He was supposed to be banished. "Why do you want him so badly?"

"Because he betrayed me. No one does that and gets away with it. I'm going to tear him limb from limb until he begs for mercy."

For the first time, I feel sorry for Octavian. Hopefully Captain Smythe never gets a hold of him—though if Octavian isn't on Crimson Ruins, where he's supposed to be, he'd better hope I don't get a hold of him either. "I don't know where he is," I say.

"No games now. You elves must have done something else with him."

"Really, I know nothing. I have as much reason to dislike him as you, if not more."

His grip tightens, and I wince. He brings my face closer to his and speaks through his perfect teeth. "Be that as it may, you could still have moved him. I want answers. *Now.*"

"I told you I don't know." I try not to let panic into my voice.

He pulls on my hair again, twisting my head around so I face Jocelyn. "George."

The group surrounding Jocelyn shrinks away, and I see her clearly. At some point, they tied her hands in front of her with a thick rope. The way they moved so quickly makes me fear what's coming. She's still on the chair, parts of her dress ripped, her eyes watering, but her head held high.

"Yes, Cap'n?" A pirate smiles eagerly, his front tooth missing.

"Demonstration, please."

"No. Please don't. Leave her alone." My wild pleas are ignored.

"Aye, aye, Captain." George's smile grows wider. He moves to Jocelyn's side. Light dances across her cheeks, highlighting the tears streaming down her face.

George places a finger on her upper arm and traces it down to her middle finger. A chirp escapes her, and I stiffen. He jams it backward with his thumb and pointer finger, and Jocelyn screams.

"No," I yell, trying to free myself from Captain Smythe's grasp. "I know nothing. I swear. Don't hurt her anymore. Please. I'll tell you whatever you want, just don't hurt her."

Releasing Jocelyn's finger, George sneers at me. I try to assess how she is, but she keeps her gaze to the ground, and it's too far away for me to get a good look at her finger.

Captain Smythe brings my face around to his again, and the chatter of the crowd picks up. "I was worried harming someone else instead of you would be less effective, but I can see I was wrong."

My neck aches from all the movement. I let the desperation I feel cling to my voice. "I know nothing of Octavian. You have to believe me."

Jocelyn's murmurs can barely be heard.

"Hmm." Captain Smythe scrutinizes me. "I hear the elves call you ugly, yes?"

I drop my gaze, leaving it unfocused. The music starts up again, and the crowd grows louder. I can't hear Jocelyn, but I try to be comforted by that fact instead of more worried.

"No answer? Surely an unsightly creature such as yourself has something to say about it. You were so beautiful before. You know, if you would have surrendered to me when I came to Sulamay Island, none of this would have happened. You'd still have your beauty, and your servant wouldn't be tortured." He pauses, as if waiting for a response, but I don't gratify him with one. "Well, let's give you and your servant a little alone time without any food and see if that loosens your tongue, huh?"

Fear strikes me in the gut. He shoves me off his lap, and I go barreling to the floor. My bottom stings, but I'm past worrying about minor pains. Aiden grabs me by the arm and drags me away from the crowd.

"Where are you taking me? Where's Jocelyn?" I keep the trepidation from cracking my voice.

"She's behind us," he says in a voice I can't read.

I don't bother hiding how relieved I am at these words. If she's coming now, they won't be torturing her anymore.

We wind our way through the room toward the edge of one corner. People become sparser as the cave narrows into a hall. The passageway is short and dimly lit with torches, and it ends in a wrought-iron door that leads to a small room. Aiden thrusts me inside, and a moment later, Jocelyn comes tumbling in after me. Grateful to finally be with her, I wrap my arms around her shaking shoulders.

"There will be a guard outside this door at all times, and I won't ever be far." Aiden's voice is curt. "Don't try anything, or there'll be a repeat of tonight for Jocelyn, only worse."

The door slams shut, and I hear the sound of a bolt sliding into place.

Chapter
SIX

⌒

I let out a relived sigh and check Jocelyn over. "Are you all right? How badly did they hurt you?"

Tears roll down her face. "I—I don't know. My finger's broken."

"I'm so sorry. This is all my fault."

Her face hardens, and her tears slow. "It is not. You haven't done a thing wrong. Why would you say that?"

"I couldn't answer Captain Smythe's questions, and…" He's right. I wouldn't be so ugly that my own mother won't look at me, Jocelyn wouldn't have been tortured, and most importantly, Constance would still be alive. I've brought this on us all. "Here—let me see what I can do about healing your wounds."

She pulls away. "No. I'm really all right. My finger received the worst of it. It's throbbing a little bit but doesn't feel so bad now."

She's probably just being brave. "If it's not bad, it shouldn't take a lot for me to heal it." I touch her before she can protest. Magic races through me. I nudge it into Jocelyn's hand and finger. Finding the strained muscles, I send some of my own health. The muscles heal, and the tingling pulls back within me until it fades in my chest.

"You shouldn't have done that." She stretches out her fingers. "Thank you, though. It feels much better."

"You're welcome. I wish I could do more. Captain Smythe said we're not going to be fed for a while, and we haven't had much to go on anyway. I'm afraid of what it's going to do to both of us."

"We'll make it somehow."

We have to. We have no other choice.

I look around the small room that's become our new prison. The floor is covered in dirt, but otherwise it's bare. If we lay down, both of us could fit lengthwise and widthwise, but that would be all. The stone walls are jagged and sinister, keeping me away from the edges. One thing about the room that offers a small amount of peace is the hole at the top. At first I'm not sure it is a hole, but then I spot a star twinkling through it.

"Look. We can see the sky from here. Freedom is so close."

"But we may never see it again. How can we keep going on like this? What can we do to convince the pirates to let us go? They didn't seem to want anything from me but to mock me. Did they want to know anything from you?"

"Captain Smythe wanted to know where Octavian is. Apparently, he's not on Crimson Ruins anymore."

"And he kidnapped you for that? No matter how important it is to him, I can't see him taking you only for that. There have to be better ways to learn of Octavian's whereabouts than capturing the princess right before her wedding. It's very odd."

I didn't have time to consider that. "You think there's another reason he took us?"

"I do, but I haven't a clue what it is."

I think about it a while. "I don't either. Nothing makes any sense."

"It doesn't matter. All that matters is we were captured, and now we have to find a way out of here. I really don't want to go back into that room. Do you know who all those people were?"

"Captain Smythe said they are his comrades. That's one reason he's so fearsome. He has an endless supply of help."

"He doesn't need them," she says. "He's tough enough without them."

I think of what she must have endured while I was still unconscious. It can't have been easy to deal with, especially alone. "You've had to go through too much to add this on top of it all."

She shrugs. "You're going through it too."

"Yes, but they're being much harder on you than they are on me. I wish there was something I could do about it." I sigh. "Do you ever wish you could be someone else?"

"Why would I want to? I don't have family, which would be nice, but I have good friends and a comfortable life. Despite all that's happened with Captain Smythe, I think I am happy with my life."

"Do you have other friends?"

"Yes. Don't you?"

I twist my hands through my skirt. I can't believe I'm still in this bulky wedding dress. I'm lucky Captain Smythe didn't rip it off me, for all the diamonds on it, though I'm sure he still has plans for them. But I'm getting off track. "I don't have other friends. There are other courtiers, but none of them are close to me like you are. I don't know how to make friends with anyone else. Tell me about yours. It will get our minds off things."

"Certainly. Kelsey is really nice. She was the first friend I made at the palace. I think she likes hanging out with me more than the others, though Joy or someone else joins us sometimes. We like to go swimming together on our off days, when the weather permits. We also go to the market and look around. We don't buy much, but we like to try things out."

"That sounds like a lot of fun." And like something I'll never be able to do.

"It is. We enjoy the time we have together."

A thought comes to me. "Are they elves?"

"They are."

Of course. I don't know of any other humans that work for me besides her. "I thought elves and humans didn't get along."

"We don't, mostly. Not many of the elves are kind to me, admittedly. They're darn right rude to me at times. But since I've been there a while, some of them have gotten used to me. That was how I was able to make friends with some of them. They got so used to having me around, and they forgot I was human. Now we can do things together without thinking about it too much."

It's nice to hear how life can be like when you make friends like normal. When you're free of restrictions placed on a princess. Especially when humans and elves can become friends. It's not a common thing at all, and one I wish would happen more. Maybe with my marriage, it will become more acceptable. If I get married. Who knows what's going to happen now?

I wish I could have more friends than just Jocelyn. As much as I enjoy her friendship, I wonder what it would be like to have that relationship with others as well.

Not for the first time, I wish I didn't have my duties, but they are what they are. I do love my people and want what's best for them. Nothing Captain Smythe will do to me or Jocelyn will change that, but I don't want to stick around and find out how bad things can really get.

We're both on the floor at our backs by this point, staring up at the ceiling, at that tiny spot that shows a star now and then.

Jocelyn sighs. "So how do we get to outside?"

Are we to be trapped here forever with these pirates? "I don't think we can. You heard what Aiden said. There's a guard outside the door, so even if I did cast a spell—though I don't know what it could be—I'd only be causing you more harm. And with him close by, I doubt I could do much, even if there wasn't a guard there. His powers are unique." I sit up, curling my legs up close to me.

She stands, crosses her arms, and taps her foot. "There has to be something we can do. I don't want to sit around and wait for them to come back. It was bad enough the first time. What else do they have in store?"

Exactly what I don't want to think about. What more will my actions inflict upon her? There has to be some way I can help instead of making things worse. "Well, let's think about the possibilities. We could…"

She stops tapping her foot and starts pacing the small space. Resting my head back on my knees, I try to think of something, but my mind is blank. The threat of them hurting her is enough to shut off my thoughts for good.

The rhythm of Jocelyn's pacing around the small room dulls my senses. My brain is panicky, but my body is exhausted. It must be the effects from the spell.

I drift in and out of consciousness. Occasionally, the sound of her distinct mumblings accompanies her movement. It seems like hours mush in and out of one another, but I don't know how long it actually is. There's still a star overhead, though not yet another new one. I can't keep track of how much I'm dozing off.

Dreams fade into reality, and reality fades into dreams. Nightmares more like. Captain Smythe torturing Jocelyn. Demanding Octavian's whereabouts. Her or me being taken away. It's all too much, but I'm so exhausted, I can't get them to stop.

Jocelyn's right. We have to figure a way out of this place, but I can't have her hurt more in the process. There's nothing we can try that's safe. We're going to be stuck in this place for who knows how long, starving, before more torture comes.

"I've got it." She grabs my shoulder.

I jump. Sleep confusion slurs my voice. "What?"

"You said you weakened the board under Captain Smythe's leg, right? And then it gave way under his weight?"

"That's what happened, but how can it help us now? The only thing not made of rock is the door, and I can't break iron."

"Not the door. The cave." She points to the jagged wall furthermost from the door, her expression lighting up.

It seems a lot harder and more dangerous than weakening a board beneath someone's leg. "I don't know. Stone is different from wood. I'm not sure I'd be able to make it fall down. Even if I did, I'm not certain we'd remain safe."

"You can do it. I know you can. They really aren't so different. This time the consequence is exactly what we're going for. I just hope it makes a big enough hole for us to get through, and that the pirates don't hear it crashing down." She raises her hands above her head in excitement.

I hold back a chuckle. "I guess I could try, but don't get your hopes up. It may not work."

"It will. I know it. You're stronger than you know. You can make this happen."

Her enthusiasm is more than I know what to do with. What if it doesn't work? Worse, what if I make the cave come crashing down on us? There are so many things that could go wrong and very few that could go right.

I'll have to make it work, though. I can't disappoint her. More than that, I don't think I can handle the pirates torturing her further. It's already been too much.

I stand. "There's something I should do first." I turn toward door.

"What's that?"

"I'm going to try to make it so this door won't open. It means that if I fail with the rock, we'll be stuck in here longer. Or crushed by rocks with no way to be rescued."

"It's better than being left in their hands." She shivers. "Besides, if this works, they won't be able to chase after us as easily. Try it."

I clench my teeth and work up all the courage I can to try and make the door stay shut. Dying of starvation with my best friend isn't the worst way to go, but not the way I want to.

Pushing doubt aside, I put my hand to the door and let my magic go to it, feeling around until it finds the edges. Once it's there, I push with all my magic and shove the edges as far as I can, trying to meld them with the rock.

"Wow," Jocelyn whispers beside me.

I pull my magic back inside and find there are no more cracks to the door. "This is it, then." I hope I didn't bring us to our death.

I take the several steps it takes to get to the back wall. I try to keep my hand from shaking while placing it on the rock. Little bits of stone dig into my hand, but I ignore the pain. I call my magic and push it outward into the rock. Feeling the weak spots closer to the floor, I press on them.

A few give way, but they don't seem adequate to create a hole large enough for us to escape through. I search for more places I can put pressure on. Everything is silent, except for our rapid breathing.

After pushing on several more spots, I drop my hand. "Get by the door," I say. Not that there's much room to maneuver around.

She obeys, and I follow. We both stare at the cave wall I worked my magic on. There's a bit of cracking. Then a little more. Then pale sunlight streams in. I barely notice the coming of dawn as I stare down the rest of the wall, waiting for it to fall and wondering if it's going to bring the entire cave crashing down on us.

There's nothing. Nothing at all.

"That's it, then." Jocelyn moans in defeat. "We're stuck here."

I slump back against the door, clenching my jaw. I didn't expect it to work. Not really. Yet a part of me hoped it would. There has to be some way to make it happen.

An idea springs to life. I slip a nearby rock into my hand, pull back my arm, and throw the rock with all my might at the stone wall. The rock slams into it and falls to the ground.

A rumbling comes from inside the wall. That doesn't sound as good as I hoped it would.

We hug the door. Dust shakes to the ground. A few smaller rocks fall down, followed by a couple more, and then even more, until half of the cavern crashes to the ground.

A few smaller rocks hit us, but most of the damage stays further. Dirt flitters through the air. I speak before it clears. "Quick. Let's get out of here before the pirates come. That was sure to get their attention."

We stumble over the pile of rocks and land on grass on the other side. The sun shines, glistening off a nearby river that runs out of a forest.

"Over there." I point to the trees.

We scamper off, not bothering to check if the pirates are chasing after us.

Chapter
SEVEN

〜

MY LUNGS BURN FROM running through the thin woods by the river. Being cooped up makes my body ache when we sprint. After some time, I slow to a walk but don't dare stop. Jocelyn hurries beside me. Our breathing comes hard while we work to replenish our oxygen supply.

We continue in silence, our pace as rapid as we can. I dare a glance back. So far, no pirates. The trees around us are nothing like I've seen before. The bark is white and looks smooth, except for black spots that jut out randomly across it, looking sort of like eyes. Tiny leaves of green and yellow litter the branches.

Jocelyn looks back. "I don't think they're following us."

"Maybe." But how could they not after the ruckus we made?

"Do you think it's safe to stop a moment and get a drink? I'm so thirsty. We haven't had any water since the pirate ship, and that seems like so long ago."

"Me, too. We'd better." I kneel beside the stream and drink. The cold drink refreshes my dry mouth and throat. When I have my fill, I lean back and wipe my lips.

Jocelyn also pulls away from the water. "That's better. My stomach is all sloshy now."

"Mine, too." I return the grin and then frown. "We'd better keep moving. Who knows how far behind they are? Do you have any idea where we are?"

"I haven't a clue."

"This is a problem. Let's walk while we think." We follow the river but stay among the trees. "We know they stopped looking for Octavian, which had to be at Crimson Island. I'm not familiar with this landscape. We must be on the north end of Bardus somewhere. Do you know anything about the area?"

"A little, from a long time ago," she says. "Things could have changed since then. If we are on the north end, the only city up here is Derelinquo Fork. There's no way to know where's it's at from here, though, other than south. There's a mountain range by it that would block us from going further south. But do we go straight south, or do we need to head a little east or west as well? I don't know, and it could be easily missed."

"We will just have to head south and hope for the best. I'm sure we can find it." We have to. We don't have another choice.

"Wait. Derelinquo Fork is surrounded by desert. If we wander too long, we'll die of thirst."

"Why is there a city in the middle of the desert?"

"I don't know. I remember something about it having a resource and being a trading town. I think they used a river."

Both of us freeze and glance at the river we're next to. My next words come out so rapidly they mush together as I walk even faster. "This has to be it, right? If we follow the river, we should be able to make it there."

"I think so. I don't remember many rivers on the northern side of Bardus."

"Let's keep going as quick as we can, then. The farther we are from pirates, the better I'll feel."

We walk side by side.

But then, I think of an obvious problem. "Since the river is easy to follow, do you think the pirates will check its path first?"

"I don't know." She looks over her shoulder, eyes wide.

I glance back as well and give a sigh of relief when there's no one behind us. We increase our pace.

"We have to try," I say. "This is the only way we know where to go."

"And the sole way to recognize that we won't die of thirst. I can't believe we're in this predicament."

I watch my feet, trying not to stumble over any of the rocks littered along the way. The few leaves under us don't give the crunch I'm accustomed to with the falling leaves in Omanska.

The day grows hotter. My dress clings to my back, soaked with perspiration. Not what I expected to be doing in my wedding dress.

As we go, I begin tearing off some of the skirt of the dress. Who cares if I'm leaving diamonds behind? I can't survive like this. Still, mother will not be happy if I leave them all, so I'm careful to mostly tear away fabric. It does make the problem of leaving a trail. Better to be fast, but just in case, I put it in the river and let it sink. At least it's a little less noticeable there.

The world around us remains sparse with unfamiliar trees. The sun slides across the sky as we stagger on, and every once in a while, we stop to take a drink from the cool stream. My stomach grumbles in hungry protest, and I attempt to pacify it by drinking more water. It's futile, though. Images of feasts spring to mind, making my mouth water.

With thoughts of food come thoughts of Constance. Tears sting my eyes. I wish I could turn back time and have her still alive. Things were better then, if not perfect. If Captain Smythe, a human, thinks I'm ugly, what must Robert think of me? Not that it matters. Not when I will be marrying his best friend once we find help and get out of this horrid situation.

But Constance—she matters. Or mattered. The ache hovering in my chest crashes in full force. The pain is unbearable. More than anything else I've ever felt. There is no relief in sight, no way to bring her back. No way to calm this torrent. If only things went differently.

"What was that?" Jocelyn rushes to my side and clings to my arm.

When did it get so dark? "What is it?"

"I heard a noise"—she points to the woods with a shaky finger—"from over there."

The crunching sound of footsteps makes me tense. I whisper, "Find a rock."

She looks at the ground, and my gaze follows. The setting sun leaves the ground dark, hiding any available weapon. More shuffling comes. I nudge Jocelyn back, away from it. Should we run, or will it call more attention? I grow lost in indecision as the movement grows closer.

Silently, we press up against a nearby tree. It may be enough to shield us in the dark. If we're lucky, and we've been anything but. Besides, we're several times thicker than the tree, and my dress is white. Or whiteish with all the dirt. I hold my breath as the movement approaches. The clang of two rocks hitting together sounds right next to us. I squint, looking for the shape of someone sent to find us.

The sunlight is all gone now. Nothing left but darkness until the moon breaks out from behind a cloud and lights up the now sun-lost world. Bathed in its light, a small creature stands at our feet. I let out a rush of air, too relieved to laugh. "What is it?" I ask Jocelyn.

"I don't know. I don't remember seeing a creature like this before."

I bend down closer to it, and she does the same. The animal's body is elongated, and it has a big, puffy tail. One thick white stripe graces the back of its black body. I wrinkle my nose and stand, and Jocelyn quickly does the same.

"It's cute." Jocelyn's voice booms though the forest after our attempts to avoid capture. Capture by a little black-and-white creature, that is. The animal stomps its feet and hisses at us.

"What was that?" I shuffle away from it.

Turning its hind end toward us, it lifts its tail, and a foul stench squirts over us. While we cough and sputter, the animal runs away.

"Egh." Jocelyn coughs. "That creature is *not* cute."

The burning stench clings to my eyes and nose. Jocelyn waves her hands wildly in front of her face and takes several steps toward the river. Through a blur of tears, I watch as she plummets to the ground. She shrieks, and I rush to her side.

Coughing against the stench, I kneel next to her. "Are you hurt?"

"I think I broke something." She moans.

Panic flames through me. That's the last thing we need to add to our journey. "What?"

Her face scrunches. "Wrist."

At least it's not something she needs for walking. It's easy to see her wrist is hanging at an odd angle. I take a deep breath and gag against the stench. No deep breathing through this.

I place both hands on the side of the injury and gently probe it. Jocelyn's eyes are closed tight, tense wrinkles forming around them. Working quickly, I call upon my magic. The tingling stirs within me, racing from my chest, out my hands and to her wrist. I search my body for health to draw on. There isn't as much there as should be, but I'm not taking any away from Jocelyn to heal her.

My magic hovers uncertainly over the wound. Her eyes flutter. Before she opens them, I finish casting the spell, fixing the broken wrist. The break mends nicely, and the tingling magic quickly dies inside me.

The lines in her face smooth out. Sitting back, I close my eyes, wearier than ever before. It eats at my strength, zapping my will to go on or even move to the stream to wash up.

Jocelyn says, "You shouldn't have done that, but thank you. I feel much better."

"You're welcome," I reply, trying to make my words clear.

Silence follows. I enjoy it for a moment, wanting to fall into a deep sleep. Instead, I open my eyes to find Jocelyn staring at me with a concerned expression. I force myself to sit up straighter. "I'm fine," I say.

She purses her lips but doesn't contradict me. "Well then, what are we going to do about this smell?"

I shrug off my sleepiness as much as possible. "Let's wash off in the river, though with the sun gone down, it may take a while to dry. I hope we don't get too chilled. We can't delay more than necessary. We need to get moving again. It will help keep us warm and—I hope—out of the pirates' reach. I fear they may have heard your scream."

"Sorry."

"Don't be. You couldn't control it."

"I'll do anything to get rid of this smell before we start again. My nose is still burning." She springs to her feet with more energy than I expect to ever have again.

She helps me up, and we take the remaining steps to the river and stick our feet in. My jaw locks at the same time she gasps.

"It's so cold." Her words pound through my head. "Maybe this isn't such a good idea. Without the sun to dry us, we'll freeze all night, even if we're walking."

"Agreed. We'll have to deal with the stench. Let's get a move on. We'll stop in a while to rest, once we're far from here."

"Egh." She coughs. "Why does that animal smell so bad?"

The burning stench clings to my nose. My eyes water to get rid of the sting. Jocelyn waves her hands wildly in front of her face, and I mimic her, hoping it will help. Nothing seems to improve at this point. We'll have to deal with it, as well as with being lost and exhausted. The heaviness of it all is eating at me, begging me to stop for the night, but we can't.

We scamper from the water and head back toward where we hope Derelinquo Fork is.

Chapter

EIGHT

❧

I DRAG MY FEET as the night wears on. After what feels like several more miles, we stop. Jocelyn's eyes are already half closed.

It scares me how sparse the trees are getting and how dry the ground is. Where will we hide if there are no more trees? "The trees are thinning. They're almost gone." My words stir some life into her, and I add, "We may as well rest here. We should move away from the river and keep out of sight."

She bounces her head up and down in agreement, and she staggers after me. We go a little ways until we find a grassy area with few rocks. The river is no longer in sight, but its gurgling can still be heard. I sit, my body sinking into the ground. This dress is horridly uncomfortable.

Jocelyn collapses next to me. "Why don't you lie down and sleep? I'll keep watch."

The idea is tempting. "You're just as tired as me, and you've been through more. I'll take the first watch."

"I've been through as much as you. I can take it."

"Why don't we both sleep? If the pirates catch up to us at this point, I don't think I can do anything to fight them off. If we are lucky enough to get some sleep, though, we may make better progress tomorrow."

"All right." She lies down. Before I can get comfortable, her breathing deepens.

It's a good thing we didn't plan to keep watch, or she'd feel terrible for sleeping through it.

I roll my body onto the ground next to her. The bit of grass provides only a little respite from the hard ground. The uncomfortable position does nothing to deter me from drifting. My mind soars like it's leaving my body to go to the land of dreams. Robert will be there, waiting to welcome me with open arms and soothe away my troubles.

His presence is warming, peaceful, and happy. It's more than I hoped I'd have until I pull out of his arms. I remember I'm engaged to another. Not just any other, but his best friend. Being in his arms isn't something I can allow myself. A chill racks my body at the thought.

A rustle to the left shoots me fully awake. The only sound is Jocelyn's rhythmic breathing. I wait for the silence to be filled with sounds of pirates. I don't know if I dread that more or another one of those horrid black-and-white creatures.

A pattering comes again from the right side of me. I sit up, no longer caring if they'll see me or not. If they're here, it's likely we'll be captured anyway. Best be prepared for it and fight it with everything I can.

I look around, trying to find the source of the noise. A squeak draws my attention. I look deep into the shadows to find a squirrel staring at me.

The little animal scurries up to me and almost climbs on my lap. I suppress a squeal and the laugh that wants to follow. It hurries away at my noise. At least I know what this creature is, though I can't help but be slightly put out that it woke me.

The night draws on, the unfamiliar world around me darkening further. Sometimes I doze, but after that squirrel startled me, every noise has me jumping back awake. An animal running past or the breeze picking up rustling the leaves. Each sound grows more ominous than the last, for my fear of pirates, but it's just my imagination running wild.

Near morning, even the rumblings of my stomach send me glancing about in a wave of suspicion. And growl it does. It aches with hunger. Everywhere I look, I see pirates and black creatures with white stripes.

When the first rays of sunlight peek over the jagged horizon, I sigh with relief. With as much effort as my sore body can manage, I nudge Jocelyn. "Wake up. We have to get a move on."

"Mmm…" Her eyes flutter open. After a few more heavy blinks, a scowl crosses her face. "I almost forgot what happened. At least I feel a bit more rested. Wait. It's getting light already." She narrows her eyes at me, sleep only partially clouding them. "How long have you been awake? You look terrible."

I suppress a flinch. It's not the lack of sleep that makes my appearance so terrible. She must still be asleep to not remember this is how I'm doomed to look the rest of my life.

"Long enough. We should take a quick rinse in the stream and be on our way," I say.

She stands with ease. "You should have woken me sooner."

She trails off to the river while I struggle behind her. My body is tense and sore, making each movement more difficult. I can only hope the pain eases as I move around, or wandering farther today is going to be a nightmare.

"You didn't answer my question," Jocelyn says. "How come you didn't wake me? If you can go with a little less sleep, I certainly can too." She steps in the river. "Ah. It's freezing."

I watch her wade out until the water touches her knees and she sits down. Suppressing a shudder, I go into the river too. A gasp rises from my lips as the frigid water freezes my toes. I take another step forward, and the icy feeling surrounds my ankle.

I clench my jaw and walk to Jocelyn. "How can you stand it? I wouldn't call it refreshing at all. At least I'm more awake now."

She splashes water on her face and then bends to dip her hair in. Groaning, I grab what's now the bottom of my dress. I rub the material together, trying to clean fast, but my hands are frozen and unfamiliar with the process. This is stupid. I rip more of it off, taking all of the underskirt. I won't have to drag it around farther. Mother will just have to understand.

She rinses off the best she can, including her ripped dress, and then moves to help me with my long hair.

Once we're done, I rush to the shore, though my skin has become accustomed to the cool water. The air bites at my skin, causing goose flesh to prick. My body shakes as I sniff to discover if the horrid smell still clings to my body. It's fainter but still there. Or maybe I'm getting used to the smell. Either way, I stink. Better to stink than to freeze to death like I'm going to, though.

"Our bodies should warm with the walking," I say, hoping it's true.

She shivers beside me. "Let's get to it, then."

We hurry along, continuing our path by the stream. In the light of day, there are fewer trees than I thought. At first it's chilly, but as the sun rises higher in the desert sky, it warms our skin with its yellow light. All too soon, it's hot, and my damp dress is sticky against my skin.

Soon, the trees are gone, and the ground is harder, growing into even more of a desert except right next to the river. My diamond-covered dress is a nuisance, heavier with each step despite the changes I've made to it. Not only that, but darkness threatens the fringes of my vision off and on, coming more frequently as time passes. Stars dance before my eyes.

"Talk to me, Jocelyn," I say, desperate for anything to latch onto.

"Talk about what?"

"It doesn't matter. Something. Anything."

"I remember when Constance first found me."

"Oh?" I perk up. Though I have a vague idea what happened, I don't know the real story. "Would you mind telling me?"

"Of course not." She takes a deep breath, like she's gearing herself up for something big. "I was eight and all alone in the world."

"What happened to your parents?"

"They died in a boating accident. I was supposed to be with them, but a friend wanted to play, and I convinced my parents to leave me behind. Sometimes I wish I'd been there with them, so we could all go together. Most of the time, though, I'm happy to have survived. I miss them to this day, but I think they'd be happy with the way my life has turned out.

"My friend's parents were kind, but they had seven children of their own. I was a burden to take on and had no other family to take me in," she says. "I know they would have supported me if they could. Their oldest was already sent out to work, and others would soon follow."

"How did that make you feel, losing your parents and being taken in by your friend's parents?" I wonder what that would be like. I have nothing in my life to compare it to. I've been fortunate enough to always have enough of everything, though I know not everyone does.

"It was the hardest thing I've ever been through. To this day, I still miss my parents. I wish they were still here. That they'd never gone boating that day."

"I'm so sorry for your loss. I wish it hadn't happened to your parents."

"It is what it is. I can't change it now, even though I still miss them. The family that took me in was kind. I knew they wanted to care for me, but being a burden like that isn't something to take lightly. Even at eight, I knew that. It made me have to grow up fast, I think. They finally decided they'd have to take me to an orphanage and wanted to find an one that would take good care of me. We traveled to the capital. I know it was hard for them to take the time to journey all the way there, but it ended up being for the best.

"As we were in the street in front of the orphanage, saying our goodbyes, Constance came up to us. I never did figure out why she was in Bardus. She got talking to my friend's parents, and next thing I knew, she was offering to take me back to Omanska with her. Said she worked for the elven Queen, and they were always in need of more workers. Said she could see to it that I'd have a good future and not an unknown one, stuck in an orphanage with so many other homeless children."

"And that's how you came to work for me?"

"Well, not at first. Constance trained me and had me practice on visitors. Once I was good enough at my job, and as soon as there was an opening, she had me become one of your servants."

"What did you think of that?" I ask, truly curious.

"I was scared at first. I mean, you're the princess of a whole nation, after all. I didn't know what to expect, but after the first day, you were so kind to me, I didn't worry anymore. I never would have guessed we'd become friends. You used to be so aloof. But something changed when we went to Sulamay Island, more so when we took that journey together afterward."

"I'm glad we had to go on that adventure, if only so we could be friends."

"And let's not forget your time with Robert," she says.

"Robert." Just thinking about him makes my chest hurt. "Sometimes I wonder... I don't know if it's better than I spent time with him or worse. Now I realize I'm to marry Abner, his best friend, being acquainted with Robert almost makes it harder."

"So you'd rather not have met him?"

"That's a difficult question. It's hard to say. I can't imagine not knowing him, but at the same time, maybe it would hurt less if I didn't. I wonder if it would be easier to keep believing he died. Not that I want him gone, but then I would know he's not even around."

She puts a hand on my shoulder. "I'm sorry it's so hard for you."

I give her a strained smile. "They're hard on us both right now."

"True enough."

She continues speaking of many things. Her voice is soothing against the grating heat. Still, the more time passes, the more I feel like I'm losing myself. My surroundings blur together in golds and yellows and oranges and heat and exhaustion. My mind is numb, my thoughts slurred.

We can't keep traveling through the desert like this. It's not safe. It's not good. We have to get out.

The world goes black and comes back.

"Arabella." Jocelyn grips my arm, and I force myself to concentrate past my dimming vision.

"What is it?" I mumble.

"We're here. We made it to the city." She dances with glee. "I'm sure someone will take pity on us and give us some food. If we don't smell too horrid. Or maybe we could say who you are. That might get you home safely."

"Unless they hate me like most humans do. I'm afraid of what their reaction might be."

"That's true. It's a risk telling someone who you are."

I drag my gaze upward. When did it get so dark? I can't remember the night coming. I can't remember much of anything, except walking.

In front of me, half covered by a rocky red hill, is a city. Electric lights waver invitingly. I take an automatic step forward.

Jocelyn grabs me by the arm and pulls me back toward the cover of a tree I didn't realize we are standing under. "Please, wait a minute."

"What is it?" I ask.

Her blush is barely visible in the moonlight. "I hate to ask this of you. I wouldn't if I didn't think there was a problem, especially because you look so exhausted—I'm afraid you're going to fall asleep standing up."

"Mmm," is the only response I can manage.

Her forehead wrinkles. "Really, I wish I didn't have to ask, but... well, I was thinking. The pirates know this area better than we do. What if they already have someone in the city looking for us? Even if they don't, someone soon will be. I think it would be best if we didn't look like ourselves. We could change clothes, but we don't have any. I think it would help if we went in disguise."

"Disguise?" I struggle to understand what's she's saying. The world swims in front of me.

"You know, the spell you did before on yourself. I was thinking you could cast it again. You'll be less noticeable here as a human, anyway. And I don't know if it's at all possible, but if you could also cast a spell on me so they don't recognize me..."

My mouth drops open, and my thoughts become a little clearer. "You want me to deform you?"

"Deform? Who said anything about being deformed?"

"Have you looked at my face lately?" I regret my harsh tone and work to explain it calmly. "You're a beautiful girl. I'd hate to be the one to ruin that."

She looks at me straight on, surprising me with the determination in her gaze. "I thought you were all right with the change. What happened?"

"I— It— I just don't want you to have to go through this."

She narrows her eyes. "Don't think I'm going to forget about this. You're different, not deformed. For now, though, I want you to know I'm not scared of any changes that may happen."

"But—"

"No, but. Can you disguise both of us or not?"

I contemplate lying, but she won't fall for it. Besides, I don't want to lie to her. "I can."

"Good. That should help."

"But what about our clothes? My dress isn't exactly easy to lose sight of."

"Our clothes will have to do as you can't change it. We'll just have to hope the pirates aren't looking for it. It does appear a lot different now that it's so dirty." She wrinkles her nose. "Maybe we can trade some of those diamonds. It's too bad we can't do anything about the smell. Let's get the magic over with, in case someone sees us on the way in."

I sigh and cast the spell on myself. The once familiar pain ripples through my eyes, cheeks, and ears, and I wonder how much more damage this will do to me.

Jocelyn nods. "Now me."

"I will have to touch you for the spell to work."

She moves closer, and we grab hands.

"I'm ready," she says.

"I'm only going to change your eyes and hair. They're your most distinguishable features. Your eyes will hurt a bit."

"I remember."

I cast the spell. Turning her hair from a golden yellow to a light brown is easier than taking the bright green from her eyes. When I'm finished, they are a soft brown, to match her hair. She still looks like herself, but much changed.

She lets out a yell. "You told us before it only hurt a little, but it felt like someone ripped the top of my eyeballs off. I don't know how you can stand adding freckles and rounding out your ears."

I shrug, weariness creeping back over me. "Sorry."

We head toward town, holding hands. It seems so far away right now, I can't imagine how long it will take us to get there. Everything aches. All I want to do is lie down and sleep for the rest of forever. Or at least until I feel better.

My mind is numb. The farther we walk, the less I take in. Dirt. Rocks. Buildings. Path. At some point, I realize Jocelyn is leading me, and the ground has changed beneath our feet.

My face and ears ache, but I dismiss the feeling. I just want to give into the darkness.

"Arabella?" Jocelyn's voice sounds far away. "Arabella? What happened to the spell? Are you all right?"

The world around me tilts and spins.

"Arabella? Not now. *Please.* Someone's coming. Get—"

Her words fade into a blessedly dark world.

Chapter
NINE

~

EVERY PART OF ME is heavy. I try to move, but nothing responds. What made me so incredibly exhausted? I remember something about Jocelyn, but that's all. Nothing more. I open my eyes and let out an unladylike yawn.

"You're awake," Jocelyn says.

I don't have the energy to respond. Instead, I search her out in the dim room. She's sitting beside my bed, worn looking, but clean. Why does the clean part surprise me? It's then everything comes back to me.

"What happened?" I ask.

Her gaze darts to the right. I follow it to find a woman not much older than me, dressed as a servant and with hair pinned back.

She gives a small curtsy and says, "I must inform the mistress she's awakened." With that, she leaves the room.

"Who's the mistress?" I ask. "Why are we here? How did we get here? Where even is *here*?"

"It's a lot to take in. I know," Jocelyn says. "We were picked up several nights ago, after you fainted. You've been pushing yourself too hard."

"I did what I needed to do." I couldn't let her go around unhealed, we had to run from pirates, and her suggestion to go in disguise so the pirates wouldn't find us was a good one.

She gives a sigh, heavy with the weight she must be carrying. "I've just been really worried about you. You've been asleep for three days."

That has me sitting up in a rush, all heaviness forgotten. "Three days? The pirates are sure to know we're here."

"They may, but we're safe for now," she replies. "After we were picked up and the man who did so saw you were an elf, he brought us here. We're at the home of the leader of Derelinquo Fork and..."

"And what?" I wonder about her unusual hesitance. Whatever it's about, it can't be good.

"She's Robert's mother."

It's not good. Not at all. This isn't how I wanted to meet her for the first time. Not that I ever imagined meeting her. It didn't seem likely to happen, and yet, here I am.

I realize I'm not wearing my wedding gown anymore, thankfully, but I'm in just a night gown. "I have to get up. Get dressed. Get presentable."

As I start to pull the bed covers off me, Jocelyn says, "Oh no you don't. Lie back down."

"Not now. I can rest later."

"She's already seen you like this; it won't be much different to have you awake. Now, you need rest, and nothing is going to stop you from getting it. Not even the ruler of this city."

"She's what?"

"Just what I said. Now bed." She firmly presses me back down.

"You've changed since I first got to know you."

She grins. "I'll take that as a compliment."

"It'd be one if it wasn't for this situation." But the bed does feel good. Too good. My eyes are already closing. "What do you know about this place?"

"Honestly, not much. Other than taking a break to clean up. I've been too worried to leave your side."

Her words touch me, bringing tears to my eyes. "Thank you for being so kind to me."

"It's what friends are for."

"Well, then, would you mind helping me put these pillows up, so I can be sitting up when she comes in?"

"Certainly."

I sit up as Jocelyn fluffs the pillows up behind me.

"Thank you," I say. "If I had to go on this horrid journey, I'm glad it was with you."

"I'm glad I could be there if you had to go through it," she says. "Next time, though, I'd prefer if we skipped it all together."

"I feel good about that plan."

"Truly, though. How are you feeling?"

"Worn. Like someone took me and my magic and stretched us as far as they could until we snapped."

"That sounds miserable. I was hoping the sleep would do you some good."

"I'm certain it has. I'm just not ready to do any major fighting anytime soon."

"And I'm not about to let you," she says. "You need more rest before we do anything else. And we're safe here for now. Or as safe as we can be."

I know what she means. Being kidnapped from my own wedding doesn't inspire confidence in my safety.

The door opens, and in comes a woman. She's tall, with nut-brown hair. Her golden eyes look familiar.

"It's so good to finally meet you while you're awake, Arabella," she says. "I am Teresa."

"It's a pleasure to meet you as well."

"Jocelyn has been rather tight-lipped about who you are and what you were doing out in the middle of the road at night."

She has? And yet she managed to get at least who they are out of them. Good for her. Is it safe enough to tell Teresa everything? I don't know. I look to Jocelyn, who shrugs. Well, this woman isn't a pirate and has been kind to us. I guess the best thing I can do is tell her the truth and hope she remains good. Like Robert.

"I am Princess Arabella. My friend and I were captured by pirates as I was about to marry your prince. Robert is an acquaintance of ours."

"Oh my." Teresa sits on a nearby chair, her eyes wide. "Robert has told me a little about you, but not much. I heard of your capture, but I didn't think we'd find you all the way out here. That explains your dress. I'm so sorry for what you've been through. Is there anything I can get you?"

"You're very kind. Thank you, but I think you've already done more than two strangers could expect from you." Just talking is making the heaviness creep in on me again. I'm grateful Jocelyn insisted I stay in bed. "I think I could use some more rest, but as soon as I'm better, I would like to be on our way if we can do so safely."

She stands. "I'll let you rest for now and go make plans for when you're ready. I'll see more of you soon." With a curtsy, she leaves the room.

"Do you need anything?" Jocelyn asks.

"Just not to be so exhausted."

"Rest, then. That'll help. I'll be here when you wake up."

My eyes are already drifting closed. I mumble a thanks, and everything goes dark.

Chapter
TEN

~∾

I'M FEELING MUCH BETTER in the morning. Refreshed, if not still a little weary. It's time to move on. I fear the pirates' retribution for staying here if they find out. They'd have a harder time since this city isn't next to the ocean, but with as great of numbers they had in the cave, I don't want to chance anything. Teresa shouldn't have to deal with them because of us. Of course, I don't want to deal with them either. I hope I never have to see them again.

I get dressed in the clothes one of Teresa's servants rounded up for us and head to breakfast. They are nice but not overly formal, and fit a little big.

"I'm sorry we don't have better clothing for you both," Teresa says.

"I'm just grateful to be out of that gown. It was atrocious."

"I thought it seemed rather lovely—if it wasn't for all the wear and tear it's been through."

"My mother would be glad to hear of your kind words."

She blushes.

"Have you met the elven queen and king before?" Jocelyn asks her.

"I regret to say I've not had the chance. I was hoping to meet them at the wedding, but duty called, and I was unable to go. Robert's father was there, though. He's still out looking for you." She looks to me. "But I've sent out notes to the human and elven castles, telling them you've been found. I did so discreetly, though, since I knew your circumstances."

"I appreciate you going to such lengths," I say. "I'm a little worried about you and possible retaliation from the pirates."

She waves away my concern. "We keep both our home and city well protected. Not only is my family important—and I consider my town important—we have a lot of goods that move through the town. If it was easy for pirates to get in, they would have by now. You needn't worry about that."

That's a load off my mind. "What do you trade in?"

"Do you know Robert well?"

I'm not sure exactly how to handle that. She's his mother after all. It's not like I can tell her the feelings I have for her son. How much more I want to get to know him. How much I may even love him.

I'm thankful when Jocelyn answers for me. "We both know him. He escorted us from the island Captain Smythe attacked us on to our home in Amara."

"You mean the castle?" Teresa's eyes glitter.

Not that we've spent a lot of time with her, but I'm getting the impression that she is impressed by riches. A memory comes back to me then—something about Robert saying his parents were greedy. His mother seems nice enough.

If nothing else, I can leave my wedding dress behind in payment. I wonder what my parents will think of that.

"Yes, we both live at that castle," I respond. "Have you visited the castle in Corona?" The human castle is one place I've been curious about, but never been able to go to.

"It's the loveliest place in all the world," Teresa says. "I lived there for a while, you know. It's airy and spacious and wonderful."

"I'm looking forward to seeing it myself," I say.

"You will love it."

"How long did you live there for?"

"A good portion of my life," she says. "How well did you come to know Robert?" She's fishing for more information about our relationship. It makes me wonder what, exactly, Robert has told her about me.

"Well—" Not nearly as well as I'd like. "I know he and Abner are best friends."

She pales. "You mean Prince Phillip."

"Yes. Right. I'm sorry. I'm having a hard time remembering."

She gains back some of the color in her face. "I suppose you are going to marry him."

Yes, I am. And somehow, coming from Robert's mother, it's a lot harder to hear.

"She is." Jocelyn speaks up for me. "So, tell us. What is it exactly your town trades in? We haven't heard a lot about it yet."

"Not heard?" Teresa looks as if she's about to go into shock. "Why, we mine the finest coal, diamonds, and silver. We're lucky enough to be situated near mines that hold them all. We ship all over the world. In fact, I wouldn't be surprised if your wedding dress was covered in diamonds from our mines."

I wonder if they were. I'd like to think so, but I wouldn't be surprised to learn they're from somewhere in Omanska. As good a way as it would be to support the cause of uniting humans and elves, I don't know if it would have crossed mother's mind. It certainly didn't cross mine. I'll have to remedy that in the future.

"Have you heard anything about the pirates' movements?" I don't really want to know, but I need to.

"They were busy around this area the first two days you were here," Teresa says. "But they have cleared out. I don't know if they are aware you are here or not, but they shouldn't cause any problems for you on the journey to the castle. I'll send you with guards in case they try something, but they shouldn't even know it's you traveling away from this city. Just another carriage on the road."

"It's so kind of you to take care of us like this," I say. "We would be happy to leave you some diamonds as payment."

She shakes her head. "I won't hear of it. I have plenty from my mines. I certainly don't need more of yours. Would you like to take the dress with you?"

"I would like to keep it"—or mother will—"but I'd rather not have it traveling with us."

"I can ship it to you, then. I'll send it to the castle in Amara."

"That would be most appreciated."

"Anything for our future ruler."

It strikes me then that I really am her future ruler. No wonder she's been so kind. I've never considered how I'll be a ruler over the humans as well as over the elves. They're about to be my people too, and I don't know nearly enough about them. The closest human I know is Jocelyn, but she grew up with us elves. I have to learn more about the humans.

Chapter

ELEVEN

～

T HE CARRIAGE IS READY," Teresa says.

"Thank you so much for everything," I tell her. "This means more to us than I can say."

"For you, it's not nearly enough."

I blush. Is it because I'm a princess, or because of what Robert has said about me?

She leads us out of the house and to a waiting carriage. The carriage is surrounded by four horsemen who will be acting as our guards, though hopefully they won't be needed—we're traveling on the back roads and inside a carriage, so we'll be hidden. We'll be able to move fast since the carriage is being pulled by four horses.

Not only that, but Teresa supplied us with ample changes of clothes, fresh things, and some money to get us through anything that may come our way. What's more, she found me a sword. I insist on keeping it with me and will the rest of my life. I don't care what anyone says; I will not be left defense-less again, even if it means being armed at my own wedding.

Teresa surprises me by taking me into a hug. "I wish I could go with you, to see you safely on, but duties require me to stay."

"We understand completely and are so grateful for all you've done for us."

"It was my pleasure."

A guard with a red beard helps me into the carriage, and Jocelyn comes in next. They shut the door, and I look out the window as we pull away. I can't help but feel a loss that we didn't stay longer and get to know Teresa better. I wave, and she waves back.

The road is more jarring than I'm used to, probably due to being a back way instead of the main route. It should take us a few days to reach the capital and safety. It feels like too long a time.

"Do you think they'll find us?" Jocelyn asks.

No need to ask who *they* are. I'm as worried about it as she sounds, though I work to keep my voice confident. "Not now. They won't be expecting us to be in a carriage, especially not with guards. We'll be fine."

She nods like she believes me, even if there's still some fear and uncertainty inside me. Captain Smythe has proved cunning and dangerous. I don't want to underestimate him.

The ride continues on and on for what seems like forever. Still less time than walking in the desert took, though. We're mostly silent. I'm too tense to talk, between worrying about pirates attacking and what's to come once I make it to the human castle. Everything is too much for me to speak.

There's a sudden lurch. I go flying toward the floor, near where Jocelyn is seated. My head bangs against the seat, and I grunt with pain.

As soon as everything is still again, I ask, "Are you hurt?"

"I… I don't think so," Jocelyn replies. "Are you?"

"It's only a bump. It's not bad." I don't think it is, though a quick brush of my fingers shows a goose egg is already forming.

The carriage door is wrenched open. The guard with the red beard peeks his head in. "Are you both well? That was quite a fall."

"We are," I say. "What happened?"

"It looks like an axle broke."

Just our luck. I scoot over and take his hand, letting him help me from the carriage onto the cracked earth.

Jocelyn hops out after me, coming straight for my injury. "It looks quite painful, but I don't think it'll have any lasting effects." She touches her fingers lightly to my forehead.

"I didn't know you understood the healing arts."

She blushes. "I don't know much."

After all this time, I'm still learning more about her.

"We can repair this," the guard says, "but it will take time."

"What's your name, sir?"

"Joseph, my lady."

Time out on the open road isn't something I want with the pirates about and looking for us. The thought of it sends a chill coursing through me. "Is there another option?" I ask.

"Yes, but it may be just as dangerous."

"What is it?"

"We could all ride horseback to the capital."

I glance at the ornate carriage that is clearly worth something to Teresa. It's too fancy not to be. "What about the carriage?"

"We could come back for it."

Being on the move is more appealing, but it would mean we'd be out in the open for anyone to see. "What do you think, Jocelyn?"

"Neither option is ideal, but I think it'd be better to be on horseback and moving."

"I agree." Though I hope against all hope that a pirate doesn't spot us.

"I'll get the horses ready," the guard says and hurries off to unhook them from the carriage.

Jocelyn and I huddle together as the men prepare the horses. It's hard looking at our broken down carriage, our way of secrecy and safety gone.

"I'm scared," Jocelyn says.

I want to fake confidence, but this time, I can't do it. There's too much at stake, especially after what she went through. "I am too," I say. "I can cast my spell to disguise myself at least."

"Not a good idea. You may be trying to hide it, but I can tell you're still weak. Besides, I know you hate the consequences of that spell. We can avoid it."

I do hate it. Having my mother unable to look at me hurts more than I ever thought it would. "We can't take the chance."

"Yes, we can." She moves forward and plays with my hair, bringing it forward over my ears.. "There. That should do it," she says.

She's gaining in confidence every day. I don't tell her my fears about the wind blowing my hair away as we ride, making my ears clearly visible. I'm too tired. "We can try it, but if we come across anyone dicey, I'm changing."

"Fair enough."

"We're ready," Joseph says.

We move over to where the horses are waiting for us. Joseph helps me on easily enough, though it takes Jocelyn several tries to get up with the help of two other guards.

Once she's settled, she gives me an embarrassed glance. "I haven't ridden much."

One more thing to cause problems. I hope it doesn't get in the way. We can't afford to slow down.

We start off all right enough. Nobody in sight for several miles. When we do pass a lone rider, he doesn't glance our way, just hurries past. Mile after mile continues to fly by.

Poor Jocelyn is slowing us down. She can't seem to get the hang of being on the horse. A guard goes over to her and leads her by the reins, but it means we have to move slower. At least we're moving.

It's growing late in the day. The sun touches the horizon, barely visible over the swath of trees we just entered. We haven't made as much progress as I'd like today, but we should stop soon. There's no point in traveling in the dark if we're not running for our lives, though it still feels like we are.

I'm about to call out to Joseph when the two guards in front of us slow. I glance around and see no reason for the slowing. They must be ready to stop as well, I think, until I realize there are lights off to the side of the road up ahead.

"What do you think, Princess?" Joseph asks. "Should we stop for the night so near to another group, or should we continue on?"

As much as I want to rest for the night, I don't dare, knowing we're this close to other people. "We best hurry on."

He nods as if pleased with my decision. "Very well."

I hope our slow pace won't draw attention to us as we pass by. As the lights grow nearer, I grow more jittery. I attempt to rein in my nerves so as to keep my horse calm.

"Whoa," a male voice calls out. "Who goes there?"

I contemplate changing, but this doesn't seem like trouble yet. I best conserve my energy. It's someone curious, not pirates. Still, the sooner we can be away from them the better.

"Greetings," one of my guards says.

"What brings you on the road in the growing night?"

"We're traveling to the captial. Anxious to be there and find an inn."

"You might as well stop," the stranger says. "You won't be reaching the capital tonight, no matter how long you travel. We're happy to share our camp."

"Thank you for the offer, but we'll travel a little longer before resting for the night."

More people gather around the man speaking with us. The group seems friendly enough, but I still don't want to stop. They may not be so friendly when they realize who I am. Not that we have to tell them, but I'd rather not go into disguise for the night, even if it's just my ears. My magic still feels worn out.

"Are you certain? It's safer staying in groups with pirates roaming about."

"Pirates?" I'm thankful the guard keeps the panic from his voice, but I'm certainly feeling it.

"They've been roaming the country, it seems. No one's sure exactly what's the cause, but it's become quite dangerous."

"Thank you for the warning." The guard glances back at me for a moment, but not long enough to draw attention. "I feel it would be best if we still moved on."

"Of course."

The man holds his torch up as the guard moves forward. The second guard is next, and I follow after, keeping my gaze down as the torchlight reaches me.

"It's an elf," the man cries out.

Joseph moves swiftly, but it's too late. Something bashes against my side, making me lose my balance. I struggle to stay upright on the horse.

"Cursed elf," another voice calls out. "You're probably what's brought the pirates down on us."

"Get her," yet another voice says.

Joseph turns around and comes back toward me, but hands are reaching for me, trying to yank me off the horse. I kick at them, but too many are grabbing at me. I fall to the ground, my horse growing skittish.

I grab the hilt of my weapon as something clobbers my back. As I stand, I pull my sword out. That stops them.

"You will let us pass," I say. "We have no quarrel with you."

"But we have a fight with you, elf."

"She's protected by the rule of the land," one of my guards calls out.

"Stupid choices aren't protected," a woman calls out.

A rock hits me on the shoulder. I grit my teeth to keep from crying out.

Joseph cuts off the crowd with his horse. "Leave her alone, and we'll leave you alone."

A second guard calms my horse, holding him still so I can climb back on.

"Get out of the way, elf lover."

I manage to get back on my horse, sword out, ready to defend myself. Though it's a bad defense against rocks flying at me. Thankfully, they hit my left shoulder, and not my right.

When my guard moves forward, I do as well.

Only that's when the real attack begins.

Chapter

TWELVE

❧

THE STRANGERS TRY to yank the guard from his horse while the other guards are trying to block the crowd from getting to me. He bashes at them with his sword while the another guard tells me to hurry. It goes against my instinct to leave a man there, fighting, but the longer I stay, the longer the fight will go.

I urge my horse forward while another rock is hurled my way. This time it strikes me in the thigh. A cry escapes me. I hurry ahead, hoping they don't throw rocks at anyone else, especially not Jocelyn.

A man steps in front of my horse. I'd like to call him an idiot for doing so—it's a dangerous thing he just did—but I'm civil enough to stop for him. Just barely in time.

"We don't want your kind here," he yells.

"Then let me leave," I shout back.

Another rock is hurled in my direction but it falls between my horse and the man. He scoops down and picks it up. I sidle my horse to the side and try to go around the man, but before I make it, he slams the rock against my leg. I kick at him, thinking I should have just ridden over him.

One of my guards comes over, and I move to the side while he makes his way between me and the man. A rock hits my guard on the shoulder with a clang against his armor.

I hurry my horse forward. If I can get away, maybe they'll leave my companions alone.

Jocelyn cries out. That stops me. I turn my horse around and race back to her side. People are clawing at her, trying to pull her down from her horse. I whip my sword toward the necks of those attacking. A drop of blood drips from one of the attacker's neck. Everyone stills.

"That is enough," I call out. "Hate me—fine—but you will not attack my companions. You will let us go unharmed. If that's not agreeable to you, I will start stabbing people, instead of just threatening to do it."

"Like you could," a male attacker says. He's next to the one whose neck I have under my sword.

That's it. I slash my sword forward, cutting the fabric of his shirt and leaving a scrape across his skin. Guilt pricks at me as I do so, but these people are too stubborn to listen. I don't know how else to get through to them. "Anyone else want to try my patience?"

The crowd is quiet now. Mercifully so. The last thing I want to do is draw more blood than I already have.

"We're leaving now, and you will let us, unless you want us to harm you. We don't wish to, but we will if we have to defend ourselves, and I promise you, if it comes to that, we will have the upper hand."

With that, I shift my horse back toward out initial direction and calmly walk him away from the crowd. My heart is galloping as fast as I want the beast to, but I don't want them to know I'm scared.

Jocelyn follows me first, staying as close to me as she can get. The guards come after her. Any minute now, I expect retaliation, but nothing happens. We make a swift but sure getaway.

Once we're about a mile away, I stop. "That was a disaster."

"I think you handled it well, like a true princess should," Joseph says.

The thought makes me warm inside. Maybe I can do something right even in a situation that feels all wrong. "I didn't want anyone to get hurt. I wanted us get away from there unharmed. I'm sorry I caused trouble." Because if I'd disguised myself, this wouldn't have happened. I should let the consequence of the spell go, but it's difficult, especially knowing how other elves react to me.

"It wasn't you who caused the trouble," he says. "Those people started it for no good reason."

Joseph moves in front of me, and we keep going despite the darkness.

I move my horse up next to his. "Do you really believe that?"

"I do."

"If it's not too personal a question, why are you so kind to me though I'm an elf? It seems most humans don't carry the same feelings as you do."

"Teresa has been my employer for many years now. She's a kind woman, who believes we are all of the same worth, no matter who we are—elf or human. She doesn't take guff from anyone who thinks otherwise. When I first came to her, I admit I was an elf hater. Shames me now to think on it. But the more time I spent with her, the more I learned that maybe you all weren't so bad. Truth be told, your magic still makes me itchy, but you don't seem to use it often."

"Not unless I have to," I say. "Thank you for telling me all that. It gives me hope that things can be different, given the chance."

"I hope they can. No one should have rocks thrown at them."

Except maybe Captain Smythe.

Chapter
THIRTEEN

⌒

W E TRAVEL WITH A LOT more caution after that, whether sleeping for the night or traveling during the day. It's not like we run into many people on the road, but every time we do, I disguise myself to look like a human. It brings me back to when I was Adelei. Though we were running for our lives just like we are now, there was a certain sense of peace that came with it.

My time with Robert. Plus Jocelyn and Constance. It was wonderful, getting to know them all better. I savor that time I had with them. At least Jocelyn is with me now, though we're both quieter than we were before. I think we feel the tension more.

"How many days' ride will it take us to get to the castle?" I ask the guard, Joseph.

"If we keep at this pace and don't have any more problems, it should take us about a week."

I hope we can be that lucky, but luck is the furthest thing from me currently. At least riding is something I'm used to doing. I continue to talk with Joseph, and Jocelyn often pipes in.

It's nearing nightfall when we hear the customary sounds of people coming up on our path. I hurry to disguise myself, Joseph watching me with an expression I can't decipher. I suppose it's strange to see if you're not accustomed to it. It's strange for me to see, and I do it all the time. Usually, I don't get to watch it.

We continue riding on, though we're cautious. Even with me disguised, I don't fully trust humans. They're going to have to change their ways if I'm to become their ruler. I'm not sure how to help them do it, but they can't keep accosting people just because they're different. If only the rumors about elves and humans didn't exist, maybe it'd be easier for us to make some headway.

When we come into sight of this camp, I see it's a small one. Not as few people as we are, but still not many. At least if there is a problem, it won't be as difficult to overcome them, but I pray we won't have to fight them. That's the last thing I want to do. Mostly, I want to eat and sleep, preferably in a nice soft bed—which isn't going to happen.

"Ho, there," a man calls out to us. "Good journey."

"Good journey to you," Joseph says.

"Where are you headed to?" The man seems friendly enough as he looks over our group. I don't trust it, but apparently Joseph does.

"We're heading to the capital. Where are you off to?"

"We're going to Derelinquo Fork. Have some trading to do there," the man says. "Would you like to join our group tonight? I've heard there are pirates about, and there's safety in numbers."

Pirates. They're still looking for me. Why is it they want me so bad?

Joseph glances over our group as if seeking approval from us all, but the way his gaze lingers on me, I know he's asking what I think.

"It looks like as good a place to stop as any," I say. We definitely want to hide our numbers with others, if pirates are about, though it means I have to be careful to keep my disguise on overnight.

"Let's rest here," Jocelyn backs me up, making it look more like I'm voicing my opinion and I'm not the leader.

"Thank you," the man says. "We're happy to have others along. I'm Chris."

Joseph introduces himself and shakes hands with him along with the other guards. We set up camp for the night, and then wind up by the fire with the others. The humans. I'm wary of them, though they don't know who I am. If I changed by accident, they could be on us in a moment.

"Tell us," a woman sitting near me says. "What are you visiting Corona for?"

"We're visiting friends," I reply.

"Too bad times are so dangerous."

"Is it always like this?" Jocelyn asks.

"Just the last several days. Don't you know this area?"

"We don't get out often," I say.

The woman gives me a strange look. "Don't you call upon your friends often?"

"Sadly, no. I've only had them come visit me until now."

"Who are your friends? Maybe we know them."

I'm at a loss. What do I do? Tell her I don't really know them that well, but they are my future husband's parents, the king and queen? I'm sure that would go over well. They'd know for certain I'm an elf then.

"Sandy and Ben Juniper," Joseph says.

"I don't know them," the woman says.

"I do," a nearby man says. "They are good people."

The conversation lulls for a minute. It's nice to sit and think without worrying what consequences my words may have.

"I miss the ease of electric lights," the woman says. "It's nicer inside, staying warm and being able to see everything."

"I miss a flushing toilet," a younger girl says.

"What's a flushing toilet?" Jocelyn asks.

"How can you not know?" the woman asks.

"These two have lived a very sheltered life," Joseph says. "That's one reason we're getting them out."

I'm more grateful than ever for his intervening.

"Well," the woman says, blushing, "a flushing toilet is like a chamber pot, but instead of having to empty it, you push a little lever, and it empties itself."

"It empties itself?" Jocelyn says. "I'd love something like that."

It does sound nice—not that I ever have to empty one, but it would be nice not to worry about someone emptying it for me. We have to bring these to Amara. I wonder how hard it would be.

"Maybe Sandy and Ben can help you figure out how to get one while you're in the capital," the man says.

I wonder what's going to happen if he mentions meeting us to them. What he'll think when they don't know us.

"You mentioned trading," I say, unable to contain my curiosity. "What type of trading do you do?"

"We get gems for trade in the market. We can make them into jewelry or sell them as they are."

"Do you have any wares with you I can see?"

The woman grins. "I'd love to show you." She gets a saddle bag and brings out several pieces of jewelry.

"They are beautiful." I'm enchanted with the artisan work done on them. One in particular, a sliver chain ending in a large oval diamond with a smaller oval on each side, is magnificent. "I love this one. How much would it cost for me to purchase?"

"Are you serious?" The woman clearly didn't expecting my offer.

"I am."

She names a price, a sum I don't have with me. In fact, I don't have any money on me; the guards have all that Teresa gave us. I look to Joseph. He gives a slight nod and fetches the required coins.

As soon as she has them, the woman passes me the necklace. I hold it up, letting the light of the fire catch it. It's perfect. I put it in my pocket to keep it safe, not wanting to wear it yet.

"Thank you. I look forward to wearing it."

"You're welcome," she says. "You're a surprising group. I wouldn't have guessed you to be the type who has money for such purchases." She eyes my clothes, and I know it's because they don't quite fit properly.

I hope she doesn't suspect us of being a band of thieves. "We had an accident recently, with our carriage. Otherwise our travel arrangements would be different," I say.

She nods, though doesn't look as if she fully believes me. "How difficult for you. Though, I must say, I'm glad you were able to stop and visit with us this evening. It's always nice meeting new people."

It's nice that she's so kind. Maybe there's more to humans than I expect. "Tell me, what do you think of Prince Phillip?" I ask.

"Oh, he's dreamy," the younger girl says.

The woman laughs. "My daughter wishes he wasn't marrying, so he'd be free to marry her."

I laugh with her. "Wouldn't that be nice?" Really, really nice for me. But then, how would our races ever come together?

"We wish he was around a little more," the man says. "The king and queen are wonderful, though."

"Oh?" I say. "What do you like about them?"

The man and the woman exchange a glance. He says, "That they're trying to unite with the elves." He looks at me like I'll start raging any moment.

Raging is the last thing on my mind. "You want us to unite with them?"

"We do."

"Why?"

"It would be good for trade."

Ah. Of course. Money. I guess it's as good of a start as any.

"What do you think of the wedding?" the woman asks. "We heard the elven princess was captured beforehand."

I try not to look at Jocelyn, afraid I'll give myself away. "We heard the same thing. It's a shame the wedding couldn't take place to unite our counties."

"You're for the marriage?" The man scoots closer, so those sitting on the other side of the fire will have a hard time hearing. "We're always wary to discuss it openly because of the hatred toward elves."

"Don't you hate elves?" I wonder how deeply they feel about this conversation.

"I admit their magic makes us nervous, but we haven't found a reason to hate them."

"I definitely don't hate them," I say. How far can I take this? "I don't even think their magic is to be feared."

The woman's eyes go wide. "Don't you worry they'll curse you?"

"Do you know anyone who's been cursed?" I ask.

"Well, no. But I haven't ever met an elf. I don't know anyone who has."

"Exactly," I say. "No one's ever been cursed. Maybe that would change if they were around more, but I think not. Otherwise, why would Prince Phillip be marrying Princess Arabella? Why would the queen and king let them be allied if it was bad for the people?"

"I heard one of the elves spelled the king and queen," the teenage girl speaks up, her voice serious. "That they've been bewitched to do as the elves want."

The man looks at his daughter. "Who have you been hearing such tales from?"

"Randy said it was true."

"Randy also picks his nose and thinks cows make water."

"So you don't believe the king and queen have been bewitched?" I ask. That rumor would explain why humans are so frightened of elves. I would be too, if we had that type of power. But most elves barely even use their magic anymore, and I've never heard of anyone bewitching someone.

"I don't," the woman says. "I think they're trying to do what's right for this country."

"The question is, what exactly is right for the country?" The words spill from my lips before I can stop them.

Jocelyn gives me a look, like she doesn't know where my thoughts are going. "It's probably time for us to go lie down. We need to get an early start in the morning."

"We should rest too," the woman says. "It was nice getting to know you."

"It was good getting to know you as well," I say.

We part ways and get ready to rest for the night.

Before I can get comfortable, Joseph stops me. "What were you thinking?" he asks, his voice low. "They now know we carry coins with us."

"Why is this a problem?" I ask.

"Because they may want to rob us."

"Oh." I guess after all that, being scared of them washed away. "We'll have to keep watch, then."

"Not we. Me and the others. You get some rest."

"But—"

"No *buts*. I shouldn't have brought this up, but I wanted to warn you to be more careful."

I think of the gorgeous necklace I purchased, the one I want to wear for something special someday, and find it hard to have any regrets. But I see his point. "Thank you for helping me learn."

"You're welcome. Now get some sleep."

Chapter
FOURTEEN

∽

W E GET UP THE NEXT MORNING, eat a quick breakfast, and say our goodbyes. I have a lot to consider over the next two days of travel. We don't run into more people overnight, though we do pass some on the road. Nobody is hostile, but then again, I'm disguised as a human so they have no reason to be.

With all the rumors of pirates, I keep expecting them to show, but thankfully, we have no encounters. The capital is a welcome sight indeed. The city is surrounded by mountains taller than any I've ever seen before. The landscape is green, though it's hard to see much of it with how crammed in the houses are. I've never seen so many houses so close together. In Amara, we let the houses breathe and become part of nature. These seem to forget nature altogether.

I make my ears rounded before we enter the city. There's no way I'm taking a chance of a repeat episode of what happened in the forest. Here, we're definitely not alone. There are people everywhere. It's a bustling hubbub of noise and activity. No matter how smooth my words or quick my sword, we'll never make it to the castle if these people realize I'm an elf.

Then again, the second group of people we ran into were nice enough. Maybe there are more of them than I expected. But that doesn't mean things will go well here. With the unknown being the major factor, I have to play it on the safe side.

Up close, the city is prettier than it seemed from afar. The people are everywhere, helping each other, trading, and talking. I'm certain there's some thieving and such problems going on as well—it's too big a city not to have such issues—but what I see is the beauty of those helping one another.

The houses are bright white and brick. Some have ivy covering them or flowers at the widows. I even see several houses with a small garden plot to the side. There's more thriving and going on than I first thought.

As we near the castle, the guards have us get off the horses. Jocelyn sighs with relief as she slides down.

I give her an encouraging smile. "You made it."

She walks toward me, all stiffness.

"Of sorts."

"I'll feel better if I never have to ride again."

One of the guards takes all of the horses, and Joseph says, "He'll bring them inside the castle. We're going a back way, to be certain you're safe."

"Safe from what exactly? More humans?" I ask.

The guards look at each other before Joseph says, "There are reports of pirates hidden within the city."

The area around us suddenly becomes more ominous. How can they be in the city, too? Don't the city guards scare them off? Our surroundings don't look so bright now. My thoughts of thieves earlier seem mild compared to the way my imagination is running wild. We can't even go in through the front door of the castle because pirates might be watching it.

Every house has corners that could be concealing pirates. Or the ivy—they could even be blending in with it. Those people talking and acting nice could be pirates, cleaned up and in hiding, looking for me.

"Let's get out of here," I say.

The guards lead us through the city until we wind through the streets from everyone. Once there's no one in sight, Joseph pushes us faster, the guards behind me staying close.

We move through the forest until we come to a spot surrounded by trees. Joseph surprises me by lifting up a piece of ground to reveal a secret entrance. I know they exist. I even know how to use some in my own castle, but to see someone open the ground before you when you're not expecting it is something else.

We climb down some stairs where Joseph finds a torch and lights it, and then we close the hatch behind us. We stumble through a corridor too small to be considered a true hall. I'm feeling a bit tight, and I'm smaller than the men are. I don't know how they stand it.

The room Joseph leads us to is small, with only four chairs and a table. Nothing else is here but the stone walls and a distant sound of water dripping.

Joseph whispers something to the other guards. One goes back the way we came, and the rest head deeper into the castle.

"They are going to let them know of your arrival here at the castle, Princess," he says.

"What about the one who went back?"

"He is making sure the way is guarded, so no one comes this way while you're here."

These men, in whose hands I've put mine and Jocelyn's safety, have thought of everything. I sit, at peace for the first time since we left Teresa's house.

It doesn't last, though. There are too many things to worry about. The pirates. My capture. Abner being Prince Phillip. Robert being alive and attacked by humans.

It's all too much.

I stand and pace the room. How long is it going to take? How many people have I left waiting like this while I did simple things like making myself look presentable? Mother always taught me presentation was key, but now I know swiftness is more important.

The wait is unbearable.

The door creaks open, and I stop my pacing in the middle of the room. Before I have time to process who it is, Robert races across the room and takes me into his arms, murmuring things so low I can't hear them.

I can't help myself. I wrap my arms tightly around him, feeling safe and peaceful. His arms are strong and sure around me. I fit perfectly against him and never want to leave. He's warm and protective.

The fears of the previous days come crashing in, and I start shaking.

"It's okay," he says. "I've got you now. You're safe. I've got you. I'll never forgive myself for telling Constance to take you away. If I hadn't, you wouldn't have been kidnapped, and Constance would be alive."

"You can't blame yourself. Not for that. Stewart was there, and he probably would have done the same thing." I cling to him harder, wishing this moment would never end.

Only it does, all too soon.

There's a scuffling near the door. Robert disentangles himself from me, though his gaze is as intense as his arms were when they were wrapped around me.

I see the reason for his releasing me. Abner—or rather, Prince Phillip. My betrothed.

No wonder Robert let go.

I shouldn't have allowed such a familiar gesture in the first place, yet I wish he was still here, next to me, saying words of comfort.

Abner—for I can't bring myself to think of him as Prince Phillip—clears his throat. I look at him, my skin heating.

"Princess Arabella, we didn't expect to find you safe in the bowels of the castle," Abner says.

I swallow past the thickness of my emotions. "I didn't expect to find myself here either."

"We know you were captured by pirates and have been searching for you since. We thought you were brought to Bardus, but we haven't been able to track you further down. We expected the pirates would have done you serious harm, but you stand before us with nothing but a bruise on your head. Please enlighten us."

Why does he sound so negative about me being here, instead of happy I escaped? "Didn't you get the note from Robert's mother?" I ask.

"My mother sent a note? The guards didn't say anything about that."

"Yes. We sort of stumbled upon her, and she helped us out." What if the pirates captured the note? "The bruise on my head has nothing to do with the pirates. There was an accident with the carriage on our escape here. I sustained no injuries from the pirates themselves, but I fear my companion can't claim the same."

"You're hurt?" Abner asks Jocelyn, more compassion in his voice than I've heard before.

She blushes. "I'm fine now. The princess healed me. It left harsh memories, but I'll manage."

"You must tell us what happened," Abner says.

I jump in, not wanting Jocelyn to have to relive anything she's not ready to. Without going into too many details, I tell them what we've been through since we were taken at the wedding. I glance at Robert only once during the narrative, knowing I shouldn't be looking his way at all. Especially not after the embrace Abner found us in. Still, I can't help myself.

His face is all hardness and concern, his lips thinned into a grim line. He doesn't like hearing this any more than I like telling it.

When I'm finished, Abner says, "We knew there was an increase in pirate activity over the last week or so, but we didn't know why. Guess I can tell my father what they're up to now. We should probably go there straight away."

The thought of having to be presented to the human king and queen is daunting. I'm not in my wedding dress any longer, but I'd feel a lot better if I could change out of my travel-worn clothing.

"Why don't we let the girls clean up first?" Robert says like he's read my mind. "They can meet us there after they've had a chance to get settled. If that's all right with you two?" he asks us.

I glance at Jocelyn, who gives a nod. "That would be most welcome." Though what would be even more welcome is another one of those forbidden embraces. I didn't know how much I felt like falling apart until he held me.

I give him another quick glance, wishing there wasn't so much that separated us.

"Guard, would you please show the ladies to two of our best guest rooms?" Abner says to a man waiting outside the room. "Once they're ready, you can accompany them to the grand hall."

"One room will do just fine," I say. "If you're all right with that, Jocelyn."

"That'd be perfect," she says.

"As you command." The guard gives him a bow before turning to us. "If you would please follow me."

We do so. The castle is lovely. The ceilings are high, and there are lots of windows, but the walls are dark stone instead of light stone, like the elven castle. There are plants everywhere, and rugs quiet our steps. We walk through several corridors before we finally stop at a door.

The guard waits on the outside while we enter. The room is very nice, if not what I'm accustomed to. There are two beds with white canopies, two dressers, and two vanities. The room has several small trees in pots and wide windows with white drapes.

I flop onto one of the beds in a very unprincess-like fashion. "I'm exhausted."

"Hear, hear," Jocelyn says.

"We probably shouldn't rest too long. Just enough to clean up somewhat. I wish we had our trunks so we could change into something clean."

"There's a basin of water over here," she says. "We can wash the dust from your face."

"And yours."

"I can take care of myself after you go."

"Except I think you should do so beforehand, so you can come with me."

"Are you sure I should?" she asks. "I'm just a servant girl."

"Nonsense. You're my best friend. We've been through too much together to be separated now." Until a thought comes to me. "Unless you'd rather not go?"

"Oh, no. I'd like to join you. I don't want to be in the way. I've never gone with you to your parents. It feels a little out of place."

"Would you feel as out of place if I made you a lady-in-waiting?"

She flushes. "You needn't go that far just to appease my nerves."

"I want to. It's something I should have done a long time ago. And it will be easier to make you marriageable, since my mother hasn't bent on the rule of servants getting married."

She tears up. "There are no words to tell you how much this means to me. Thank you so much."

"You're welcome." I hand her my handkerchief. "Now let's go down and meet the king and queen. I have to admit I'm rather nervous myself."

"What for? You've met them before, haven't you?"

"Sort of. They've been at a few official functions, which I was present at, but we never did more than exchange pleasantries. They were at the wedding, but I didn't really see them. I was so focused on what was to come." Who knew it'd be kidnapping by pirates that would lead me to be all the way over here?

"Suppose that means we're going into this together."

There's a crash, and something comes flying through the window. Jocelyn screams at the same time the door swings open.

The something is a someone. A pirate. And he's running at me, with a sword in hand.

Chapter

FIFTEEN

❧

I PULL OUT MY SWORD, unwilling to be taken again without a fight. The guard comes running in. As the first pirate reaches me, a second and third come in through the window. My sword meets my opponent's with a clang. The guard is there next to me, stabbing toward my attacker's unprotected stomach. My attacker shifts his blade to block it.

Before I attack again, the second pirate is on us.

"Jocelyn, get help." I don't turn to see if she's following orders. If she can, she will.

All three attackers press in on me and the guard. I'm not used to so many swords coming at me, all at once. I slash at them, hoping help arrives soon.

Still, they press on. My guard takes a cut to his arm. I fend off a cut of my own. Magic is needed to make this fight one we can win. Otherwise, the tides are quickly turning in the attackers' favor.

As I parry another attack, I try to think what could help. It's not like we're outside. Though a window is open, I doubt it's enough to have any of Mother Nature's help. It's too late to disguise myself.

What I need is a spell like the one I used on the pirates before. A type of electric charge. Problem is, I don't know how I did it in the first place. What's more, they have to be touching me for it to work, I think.

A sword swings close to my legs. I'm too focused on magic instead of on the fight. I jump back, and then press all my weight forward in a lunge, thrusting my sword toward my attacker's chest. It hits. I try not to think too hard about it as I pull my blade out of the area below his right shoulder. There's not time to think. Another attacker is coming.

With blood dripping from my sword, I block three angry blows. Dancing around his sword, I thrust my own at him, trying to make contact with something vital or something distracting.

My guard is fighting with the other attacker, and the one I stabbed is still on the floor, though he's trying to crawl to the window. I force myself to ignore everyone but the man attacking me.

Our fight is fierce and dangerous. He swings close to me several times, but I always block before he can stab me. He aims for my non-vital parts, which helps. My shoulders, my arms, and my legs. It's harder to defend my appendages when I'm accustomed to protecting my core.

He swings at me again, and I block. He moves so quickly, it's hard to follow his every action. I'm relying on training and instinct more than anything else. They can't fail me now when so much is at stake.

I thrust my sword, feigning moving toward his chest. At the last moment, I swish to the side and cut his hand. He drops his sword with a cry.

Blood drips from his hand as I hold my sword at the throat of my attacker, ready to lunge forward if he makes even the slightest move. "Where's Captain Smythe?"

"Like I'd tell you, even if I knew."

I pinch my lips together. "There's certain to be someone here who's more... shall we say *persuasive* than I am. You'd be much better off telling me now, than dealing with them."

"You threaten me with torture?" The pirate cackles. "Nothing you can do would be worse than what the captain will do if I betray him."

I give up questioning him further, having seen a small part of what Captain Smythe is willing to do for myself. His men would know better than me what he's capable of.

By the time the guard reaches me, my arm is shaking. Not from the strain, because there isn't much of one, but from the memories. Fighting and blood and Constance.

It's all too much.

A hand pulls me back by the shoulder.

"They've got it now," Jocelyn says. "You can put your sword away."

It takes me four tries to get my blade in its scabbard; my hands are still shaking so much. I look closer at the attackers now that we aren't fighting. The state of their clothes and filth confirms they're pirates as I thought. Why does it always have to be pirates? Why are they attacking me in this very castle? I'm not safe anywhere.

Jocelyn pulls me out of the room, away from the carnage and the pirates' watchful eyes.

The hall is oddly quiet after the ruckus of before. I grip the hilt of my sword, unwilling to let it go despite the blood dripping from it. I'm unwilling to let anything else happen.

"Are you all right?" I ask Jocelyn.

She lets out a shaky breath. "As well as can be expected. I hope they catch Captain Smythe soon, so this can all be over."

Whenever it is, it won't be soon enough.

Chapter
SIXTEEN

⁓

W

E MOVE TO ANOTHER ROOM, clean up, and it's time for even more guards to escort us to the king and queen of Bardus. I hope the encounter is one of peace and calm and nothing like the fray we just left.

I let out a deep breath. "Let's do it, then."

Jocelyn opens the door for me, and a servant leads us down several increasingly ornate halls until we arrive at an intricately carved door. I'm too fidgety to pay attention to the details.

Jocelyn puts a hand on my shoulder. I give her a weak smile.

And then it's time.

The servant opens the door, and we walk inside, Jocelyn a few steps behind me and to my left. I wish she was right next to me. Better yet, that our positions were reversed. Not that it would help our people as much. But if that was the case, I would not only be free from having to perfectly represent my country right now, but also free to be with Robert.

Such thoughts are useless, though.

Robert's the first person I notice as we enter. He's on a chair on the dais. Why would that be? Maybe as Abner's friend? As his protector? Whatever the case, he's on the lowest chair, next to Abner on the very end. The king is in the highest sitting chair next to Abner, followed by the queen, whose chair is about as high as Abner's. An empty chair stands to her other side.

The four of them look so regal. I wish I had better things to wear and wasn't just in a fight.

I walk forward and give a curtsy. They each bow or curtsy back to me before sitting back down. Two men appear, holding chairs for Jocelyn and me. I relax into mine as gracefully as I can, but I want to plop down like a commoner. Manners shouldn't be required after the ordeals we've been through, but such it is.

"Welcome, Princess Arabella," the king says. "And your companion is?"

"This is my lady in waiting, Jocelyn Olsen."

The King raises his eyebrows at this, and it's then I realize my first lady in waiting is a human. Good. I hope it sends a statement not only to these we're before, but to people across both our lands. This bickering has got to stop.

"We heard you've been in much danger."

"Yes, your Majesty. I'm afraid our arrival here for the first time is not what I would want it to be."

The king leans forward. "We have the pirates who attacked you in prison. Unfortunately, we have no way of knowing who the people were who attacked you on your journey here. We're so sorry our people behaved as such."

"It's not your fault they behaved in an unbecoming manner," I say. "Hopefully, with our continued cooperation, incidents like this will become fewer until they're gone."

"We hope for that as well," the queen says. "It's a shame rumors abound about your people here. Having known your parents for some time, I know what people say is not true. It would be a shame for our people to miss out on all that you have to offer."

"We're doing everything we can to dissuade those rumors," the king says. "A note has been sent to your parents. We sent it as soon as we heard from Phillip that you were here. They should have it soon."

"Thank you," I say. "I don't want them to worry about me more than they already have."

"Of course. And now that you're safe, we should make arrangements to have the wedding rescheduled."

Abner takes up the corner of my vision, almost burning it, but I force myself not to look in his direction. "That would be a good first step in getting the people to understand we're serious about putting our two nations together. Especially after being thwarted by pirates. They need to know how sincere we are."

"We agree," the king says. "To that end, we are gathering things to be ready to leave in the next two weeks. That should be enough time to hear back from your parents and make certain they know we are coming. We will have to also make arrangements concerning your safety, both in the meantime, and at the wedding. We'll do all within our power to make certain no one harms you or takes you again."

The words would mean more if I hadn't been attacked in their very castle. At least now they'll know they need to be on guard, even in their home. "Thank you," I say.

"Now," the king says, "Phillip has requested some time to speak with you. I'm certain you have much to discuss, and now you'll have time to get to know one another before your marriage. Make good use of it."

The last thing I want to do is make good use of time with someone who lied to me about something as important as Robert being alive. Still, I don't have much of a choice at this point. If I can get him away from his parents, though, I'll be able to tell him my true feelings. Or yell them at him.

Prince Phillip, or Abner as I still think of him, makes his way out of the room. Robert moves to follow, but he stops when he gets to Jocelyn and me and motions for us to follow Abner. We do so, my anger growing by the moment.

Once we're in a private room, away from the king and queen, I feel at liberty to let my emotions out. "What, exactly, happened with you lying to me, Abner?" I demand. "I have a right to know."

Abner and Robert exchange a glance. Like that will fix anything.

"I was stupid," Abner finally says. "Beyond stupid. I was angry and hurting over my best friend, but that's no excuse for my behavior."

"If I'd known what he did, I would have sent word," Robert says. "I didn't know he sent a line about my being dead, and I didn't feel like I could send you a note for no reason."

Even with a reason, notes between the two of us would be considered bad form. Still… "How about a *thanks for saving my life*? As startling as getting a note from a dead man would have been, it would have been preferable to what I've gone through." Anger simmers in my words.

"I admit it's what I should have done. But I didn't. I was an ungrateful cad."

"You were," I say halfheartedly.

"Can you forgive me?" Robert asks, voice soft.

Like that's a hard question. I wish it didn't need to be a question at all. "I can forgive you, especially since your role wasn't a big part of the problem. It's this one"—I jab my finger at Abner—"who should have known better."

"I do know better," Abner responds, face drawn. "I should have never done such a thing."

"You shouldn't have." My anger is fading. I want to keep it bright and hot, but this is the man I'm to marry, Robert's best friend, and the person supposed to help me bring elves and humans together.

"What can I do to make it up to you?" he asks.

"You can start by never lying to me again," I say, my temper already cooling, though I haven't entirely forgiven him yet. I will, but it's not an easy thing to do.

"I definitely won't act out like that again. You can rest assured."

"And you can be nicer."

His nose flares, but then the tension leaves his body. "You're right. I can be. I guess I believed the rumors about elves a little too much, but spending time among you has changed my perspective about what you do and don't do."

That's a lot more than I expected. A good step in the right direction. "It means a great deal to me to hear you say that."

"Now we have that settled," Robert says, "can you tell us more about what you went through? We both feared the worst."

I glance at Jocelyn. "It wasn't death, but it wasn't good either. Are you certain you want to hear the details?"

Robert clenches his jaw.

Abner says, "We need to know the crimes Captain Smythe committed, so we know how to best handle him when he's arrested."

When, not *if*. It feels more like an *if* though. Captain Smythe has eluded capture this long. What's to get him captured now? "The first thing you should know is Captain Smythe isn't working just with humans anymore. There was an elf with him. One with powers I've never seen before."

Abner squints at me.

"What type of powers?" Robert asks.

"He could nullify my magic. I don't know for certain, but I think he may be able to stop any elf's powers simply by touching them."

"That doesn't sound good."

"No, it doesn't. The other thing about the elf—Aiden—was that he seemed skilled in more than one area, like me. We saw him stop my powers and change the movement of water. He could be hiding more."

"This bodes ill."

"I don't know," Jocelyn says. "While he did everything Smythe ordered, he didn't seem too happy about it. When the pirates started badmouthing elves, he looked down right livid. I wonder if Smythe is holding something over him."

"That is worth considering," Abner says. "If he is, we may discover a way to stop him."

"Who we really need to stop," Robert says, "is Captain Smythe. He's been a source of too many problems."

"He also has a cave full of supporters." I describe the cave and its location as best I can, with Jocelyn throwing in help when needed. "I can't help but think he's making his own little town that will follow his commands."

"We're going to have to change that," Abner says. "And we're going to have to capture Captain Smythe."

"But if he hasn't been arrested before now, how are we going to manage it?" I say.

That silences everyone.

What are we going to do?

Chapter
SEVENTEEN
∾

T HE NEW DAY COMES, brisk and unwelcoming. Even with the added security, it was a fitful night of sleep. Every little sound had me reaching for my sword, but nothing ominous happened other than a lack of rest. I wish I was in my own bed at home. Of course that can't be until things get more settled down.

I manage to get ready, though not without difficulty. It's not something I'm accustomed to doing myself, but I don't want to wake Jocelyn or ask a servant for help. Once dressed, I make my way out in the hall to scout out my surroundings.

It's odd being in a new place that reminds me so much of home and yet is so little like it. This palace is covered with pictures and decorations just like my castle. They're both made of stone, though this one is more of a grey instead of white. Our palace is airy. Even with the tall ceilings, this one feels closed in.

My guard follows along silently as I explore. We run into a girl about my age. She's beautiful, with thick black hair and dark eyes. Her skin is pale, like an elf's. If she had pointed ears, she could pass for one.

"I was hoping to find you," she says. "I'm Princess Belle."

I give her a curtsy. "It's good to meet you."

"And you as well. Phillip has spoken much about you."

"He has?" The thought makes me nervous. He doesn't seem to like me at all. What good things could he possibly have to say about me?

"Well, mostly about his impending doom of getting married, but I'm sure that's changed since he's gotten to know you."

Or not. If anything, it's probably made it worse. I can't think of a response.

"Oh, I said the wrong thing, didn't I?" She brings a dainty hand to her mouth. "I always seem to be doing that. I didn't mean to make it sound like you're his doom."

I smile, warming to her despite her words. Maybe even because of them. "It's all right. I don't mind at all. I'm about as happy at the situation as he is."

"I can't imagine how you must feel, being betrothed. I'm grateful my parents are letting me pick my spouse."

"They're letting you pick?" That's strange for the person second in line for the throne. I would expect another political match.

"Yes, well, I'm not all they thought I would be. I'm not even all I thought I would be. You see, I'm not exactly the type of person that does well with politics. With never managing to say the right thing, I put myself into trouble. That's not something most high-ranking men want in a wife."

"I'm sorry." I'm at a loss; what else is there to say? I thought I'd want to be like her, but hearing her describe her position makes it sound even less desirable than being promised to a husband I hardly know.

"It's all right. I don't mind at all. I only wish my parents didn't mind either."

I think of what it's like to not have my mom unable to look at me since I appear more like a human. It hurts. I want to be close with my mother, and this puts up a barrier between us. "I know what it feels like to not meet your parents' expectations," I say.

"No one's life is perfect, I guess."

"For not saying the right thing, you sure know how to respond."

"For now." She giggles. "It won't last. And you might as well know that, if we are to be sisters."

Sisters. I've never had one before. The closest thing I have is Jocelyn, but I can't see my relationship with Belle being that close. "I like the sound of that."

She smiles up at me, like I just made her day. "I'm glad. What are your plans for the day?"

"I haven't decided. Something that involves not being attacked by pirates would be preferable."

"That sounds like a good start. How would you like to accompany me through the day? I have a few responsibilities I need to take care of, but they can all be done with your company."

"That sounds lovely."

Belle starts down the hall, and I go with her.

"First, I have a meeting with some people to plan a party for my mother's birthday. It's not for a while yet, but she's earned it," she says.

"Birthdays are lovely events."

"Especially this one. Mother is old."

I barely keep myself from laughing. "I'm sure you'll make it a wonderful event for her."

"I hope so. After all the wedding stress, she deserves a great bash."

"I didn't realize the wedding was stressing her out so much," I say.

"Oh, that was something I probably shouldn't have said. Or I should have worded it differently. It's only that there's a lot of pressure on our two countries."

"I know. There's a lot of tension."

"You'd know better than most, I suppose."

"Unfortunately, I do."

We turn into a room, where a group people are waiting for Princess Belle—all human. They watch me with everything from strained reserve to hostility. A few look at me curiously. Mostly, I feel like I should have stayed in bed, like Jocelyn chose to.

"Everyone," Princess Belle says, "thank you for meeting with me today. I'm hoping we can accomplish a lot. I'd like to introduce to you the elven Princess Arabella."

Those gathered break down into curtsies or bows. While some genuinely dip, others are stiff. Those are the ones I want to avoid if I can possibly manage to do so. The way they glare at me as they stand back up, I think they want to avoid me just as much.

Belle speaks with them in small groups. I make myself as tiny as I can in the corner. A princess should command a room—that's what mother says. Right now, it doesn't matter that I'm royalty.

The time passes more slowly than ever. Captain Smythe could probably learn new torture techniques from these people, and they don't even have to touch me. They just send their dagger of a stare my way. I pretend not to notice, but there's only so much pretending one can do.

Finally, one of the group makes their way over to me. A woman of grace and beauty, in her thirties. She's wearing a refined gown.

She curtsies to me—a real bow, not a stiff, angry one. "If it pleases you, I would like to speak with you."

"Of course." It had better not be something I can't handle.

"What happened between you and our prince? I heard that pirates attacked you and stole you away, but I also heard…" She pauses. "Well, I've heard a lot of things, and I wasn't sure what to believe."

Trepidation fills me. "What type of things?"

She turns red. "Just *things*."

"Like what?" I don't like to be pushy, but I want to know what the humans are saying about the wedding that was supposed to take place and didn't.

"That you backed out of the wedding and ran away," she says in a rush. "But I didn't believe it. At least, not when I saw you here. It made me curious about what really happened."

That's what people think? That I ran away? It's a tempting thought, but one I would never carry out. "I didn't run."

"I didn't think you did." Her voice grows smaller. "Not any longer."

I inwardly sigh. If I tell her, word around about my real experience will get around and stop these rumors that I ran. Sheesh. No wonder people here don't like me. "Captain Smythe showed up at the wedding and stole me away," I say.

She gasps, drawing attention from others around us. "Not *the* Captain Smythe."

"The one and only."

"How did you escape?"

A man and a woman creep in closer. I tell my story, downplaying my own part. I know how much they hate magic, so I hesitate when I come to that, but in the end, I decide it's best to tell them.

Instead of upsetting them, it brings more people over, until even Princess Belle stops what she's doing to hear the story.

"And that's how I ended up here," I finish.

The woman who first came up to talk to me has her fingers on her lips. "Oh my. You are so brave."

I shrug. "I did what I had to do to survive."

"And modest too."

"You're nothing like I expected the elven princess to be," a man says.

I don't know whether to take that as a compliment.

"You're better than I thought you would be," another man says.

"Will you start over?" a woman in the back asks. "I didn't get to hear the whole thing."

So I repeat my story. Others come in the room and stop to hear it as well. I'm glad I'm used to being in front of people, though not used to them looking at me like this—without disgust on their faces. That's how elves look at me now. It makes me not want to leave the humans.

"Thank you for sharing that with us," Princess Belle says when I've finished for the second time. "It was most enlightening."

"I had a lot of help along the way."

"Of course you did, dear," the first woman says to me.

The crowd fizzles out, most leaving the room to do who knows what other duties.

"Not what I expected when I had you come with me," Belle says.

"Not what I expected either," I reply. "I hope I didn't take away too much from your work this morning."

"Oh, you did."

My face falls.

"Oops. I didn't mean it like that. I meant we didn't get as much done as I thought I'd be able to. It was well worth it, though. We should take you around the palace to entertain more courtiers."

I laugh. "I think I've had enough of interrupting your activities for one day."

"Nonsense. It's been a refreshing change of pace," she says. "Besides, if we're to be sisters, we should be getting to know one another better. What do you say we go eat now? We'll have it in my sitting room, the two of us. No interruptions."

I smile up at her. "That sounds grand."

Together, we go to lunch. I can't help but like her more the longer we're together. If I ever had a sister, I would want her to be like Belle.

Chapter
EIGHTEEN

⌒

W HEN MY TIME with Belle is over, not just
lunch but several hours of spending more time
with her, I make my way back to the room I
share with Jocelyn.

She's up and moving about when I enter. "Why did you let
me sleep in?" she asks.

"Because you never get to. I figured it was about time for
that chance."

"Well, thank you. "

"You're welcome. You should do it more often."

"It feels right that if you have to be awake I have to be
awake too."

"You're the only one who thinks so." And, well, my mother,
but this is one case where I don't think my mother is right.
Jocelyn is as much a person as I am, and she deserves to be
treated as such. I wonder if I can get my mother to see this.

"I had word while you were out," Jocelyn says.

"Oh? What was that?"

"Andries is here."

He is supposed to have the scroll I found back in the cave, on Sulamay Island. Maybe he has news. More than that though, I worry about how I'm going to break news to him about Constance. "I have to go speak with him," I say.

She smiles at me like she knew that was going to be my response. "We have dinner with the royal family in a little while. I don't think there's time now."

And dinner will last until well into the evening. I won't be able to bother Andries tonight. "I'll go first thing in the morning, then."

DINNER IS A MUCH LOOSER affair than I'm accustomed to. The king and queen eat at the same table as everyone else, though it may be because there are very few guests. It's the royal couple, Abner, Belle, Robert, Jocelyn, and me. It's a fine, small party, to be sure, but even so, my parents would have a separate table for them. Possibly a separate table from me as well, depending on who was coming and how they felt.

I remember the ball I attended that was supposed to be in my honor. I was shoved in the corner of the room because of my face. I don't know what to think about that, especially with being so accepted here. It makes me feel worse about the way my own parents treated me.

But I don't want to entertain such thoughts right now. I want to enjoy my meal.

"Tell us, Arabella," the queen says, "what are the latest fashions like in Omanska?"

"Truthfully, I don't keep up with them very well. My mother would be a good person to talk to about such a thing. She designed my wedding gown."

"It was such a beautiful thing. A pity that it was ruined."

I can't claim I'm sad over the loss. Instead, I say, "You will have to trade details with her when you next see each other."

"I would love to do so."

Earlier, Belle said the wedding stressed her mother out. I look for signs of it but see nothing. Though she has more wrinkles than my mother, she's aged gracefully.

"Phillip," the king says, "what plans do you and Arabella have for after you're married?"

My face heats.

"We haven't," Abner starts. "That is to say, there hasn't been a chance to discuss it."

"I suggest you get right to it," the king says. "You haven't much time left, you know."

"Yes, Father."

"What about you, Arabella?" the queen asks. "Have you given much thought to what you want to do with your life after the wedding?"

I feel Robert's gaze on me. Everyone is looking at me, so I don't know why I feel his so keenly. "I haven't given a lot of thought to it, but I would like to find a way to help unify our two people. Phillip and I will have to talk about it, but maybe we could go on a tour of both our counties."

Abner nods. "It would be good for the people to see us together like that."

Whatever happens, I hope Abner doesn't decide that Robert needs to come with us. The two of them stick together so close, but I can't imagine having to spend time with Robert once I'm married. It's hard enough knowing I'm going to marry another. I suspect it will be worse after the fact.

Dinner continues in much the same way. Questions are asked that border on awkward but never cross the line. I'll give Abner's parents one thing—they know how to get acquainted to a person. It's a skill most handy when having to lead a nation.

Following dinner, the men retire to one room while women go to another.

"If you don't mind me asking," I say, "why do you separate the women from the men after dinner?"

"Oh, I don't even know anymore," the queen says. "It's been a custom as long as I can remember. I think we could get rid of it now, if we wanted, but sometimes it's good to have an excuse to have some girl time. Don't you think?"

"I do like the sound of that." I wonder what Mother would think of it. Having alone time with just the girls. Just her and me. I'd like to get to know her better one-on-one like that, but I doubt she'd be willing to try. At least not after dinner when she either meets with guests or starts her beauty routine. I'll have to find some other time for us to get together.

We sit in a well-decorated room, and the queen says, "Jocelyn, how long have you been a lady in waiting?"

Jocelyn gives me a glance. "Not long."

The queen stares at her, as if waiting for a more direct answer. I don't want to answer for Jocelyn, but I do want things to go smoothly.

"I became one when we got to the castle," Jocelyn says.

"I must say, that's not what I expected at all. You behave like the perfect lady in waiting," the queen says.

"Thank you."

"Certainly. I'm more lax with my own ladies in waiting. I used to take them with me everywhere I went, but then I got tired of having someone follow me around all the time."

I eye the guard who's been tracking my every footstep. Usually I try to ignore him, but it's not easy. "I know what you mean."

"Tell me of the customs in Omanska. What is your favorite holiday?"

Jocelyn's face lights up the same way my chest does. Nothing is better than holidays.

"My favorite is probably Osay," Jocelyn says, her smile bright. "I used to love becoming a royal for a day when I was a child. It was wonderful that I worked in the palace because I had access to better clothes than most on Osay."

"I didn't know that," I say.

She blushes. "I like fine food and clothes. What can I say?"

The queen laughs. "Don't we all? And what about you, Arabella? What is your favorite holiday?"

Most holidays I'm expected to do things like stand forever in hot, uncomfortable dresses, I can't say they're my favorite time, though there are a few I do enjoy. "Omanska Day is probably one of my top days. I love celebrating my country and people."

"Very good choice."

"What about you, Your Majesty?" Jocelyn asks. "What is your favorite holiday?"

"I prefer Ilym, when families get together to just be families. I do enjoy the time I get to spend with my son and daughter."

"And here I am, taking your son away," I say.

"I'd like to think that, instead of taking him away, you're adding yourself to the mix. I'm looking forward to seeing you next Ilym."

I smile, truly happy. "You know I'll be there."

The men come in the room, and the queen says, "Oh, just what I wanted." Her expression gives nothing away, but there's a twinkle in her eye.

The king walks around the back of the sofa and lightly touches the queen from one shoulder to the other before coming to rest in his own chair, across from us. If I hadn't just witnessed that act, I'd think he didn't care much for his wife.

The rest of the night, I keep an eye on the whole family. They're not open with their love, but they're open with their closeness. If they're this way all the time, it's a bonus in the family I'm marrying into.

If only I could bring myself to love the groom.

Chapter
NINETEEN

❧

THE NEXT MORNING, I wake early. I dress and try not to wake Jocelyn. She didn't sleep well last night. I woke several times to her calling out for help. I'm afraid she's having nightmares of the pirates' cruelty. She deserves to sleep in while she finds some peace in rest.

When I get out of my room, I'm ready to find Andries. I'm eager to discuss things with him. Well, *some* things. I have to tell him about Constance, in case no one has yet. It's not a task I look forward to, but it needs to be done. I ask my guard for directions to where I can find Andries if he's awake this time of day.

"Andries is always awake," the guard replies. "He lives in the library, for all intents and purposes."

"Would you take me there?"

"Yes, my lady."

We've walked through several hallways when Belle crosses our path.

"You're up and about early," she says. "What are you doing?"

"I'm going to find Andries."

"Oh, the eccentric elf." She puts her hand over her mouth. "I mean, the nice elf who's been here for a while."

I laugh. "Yes, him. I haven't met him, but *eccentric* sounds about right from what I hear."

She blushes. "I'm glad you're different than the other courtiers."

"Me too."

"I really do appreciate it. Most others aren't kind to me when the wrong thing comes out of my mouth."

"We all say things we don't mean at one time or another."

"Yes, but not as bad as I tend to," she says. "I'm glad you're the one marrying Phillip. I'd hate to think one of these horrid courtiers would marry him instead."

I can't answer right away.

Before I get around to it, she says in a lowered voice. "You don't want to marry him, do you?"

I shrug. I don't know her well, so I'm not sure how much to trust her with. At the same time, she's so sweet and eager, I can't imagine her doing anything bad with information that feels as if it's common knowledge. Besides, if we're going to be sisters, I may as well start by being more open.

"It's hard marrying someone you don't really know," I say. "It's not something I would have chosen for myself."

"I can only imagine how hard it must be for you."

"Yes, well, I'm hoping to get to know Abner better, and that should help." Not that I want to spend more time with him. As much as I shouldn't be, I'm still bitter about him lying to me about Robert dying.

"We're as different as siblings can be, but he's got a softer inside than he lets people know about."

Wouldn't that be nice? I don't want to spend my marriage with a stranger. It's hard to imagine anyone willing to spit on a princess as having a softer side. "Thank you for your kind words," I say.

"Well, I leave you. I have some duties I need to attend to, anyway."

"It was lovely seeing you again."

"You as well."

She's off with a flounce, and I continue on to the library.

Inside, it's filled with books farther than I can see. There's a man sitting at a table and surrounded by books and scrolls. He's older, but aged well, and definitely elven, with his finely pointed ears. His silvery hair is short against his tanned skin—a tan I've never seen on an elf before—and his eyes are a vivid blue behind reading glasses.

When he sees me, a smile crosses his face. "You must be the princess Arabella."

"I am. I've been looking forward to meeting you."

"And I you. I've heard a lot about you." At least some things from Constance. I wish I could have heard more. "Would you like any news from Amara?"

"I have to admit, I was hoping you could tell me about a certain person."

Constance. Pain surges through me. If only they'd been together all these years... How am I ever going to tell him?

"It's not good news, is it?" he asks.

I shake my head. "I'm afraid—" My voice catches. I swallow past the thickening in my throat. "I'm afraid Constance is no longer with us."

The light in his eyes is snuffed out. My heart aches. She should be here with me now, reuniting with her long-lost love. Instead, she's gone because of Captain Smythe's cruelness.

"What happened to her?" he asks, voice cracking.

"She was sticking up for me. Trying to save my life." Tears come now. I couldn't stop them if I wanted to. "When the pirates tried to take me away, she demanded they release me. Captain Smythe took her life."

His fisted hands shake at his sides. "That man has destroyed more lives than one person should have control over."

Don't I know it? I want to pay the pirate back, but there's no way. He's too strong and has too much power over too many people. Maybe I should have fought harder. Tried to do more, even though Aiden was there. Jocelyn's life was in the balance too, but how many more people will be hurt by him because I didn't do more?

"I'm sorry for your loss," I say. It's not nearly enough.

"As I'm sorry for yours. I know how much you meant to her."

It meant so much that she was willing to give up her true love to be with me. The thought makes me feel guiltier than ever.

"There's some news for you on the scroll," he says, though his heart isn't into what's before him like it was previously.

"What's that?" I ask.

"I was unable to uncover some of the words and traced the scroll back to a woman believed to have the sight of fore-telling. Why don't you take a look?" He pulls out the scroll and holds it up for me.

The sight? That's rare, even in olden times when magic was more plentiful. I read with eager eyes.

> *My people ache to have a leader who is wise. Instead, they are yanked apart by greed and un-happiness. The one hope is that it shall not last forever, for I have seen the sign I have wanted for. Many years hence, there shall be an elven princess of pure heart. She will wed a human prince with a heart full of love and care.*
>
> *The two will unite the people, and peace will again abound.*
>
> *As I sit in my cave that is now home, rocking my baby, I can't help but think it will be too late for us. I climbed Mount Incidium, hoping for*

It's more than I thought I would hear. It describes my present, my people and humans being pulled apart by unhappiness. I have hope this will happen, that wedding a human prince will untie my people, and we will have peace again. Only, I fear I'm not pure in heart, like it says. There has to be more than a little hope for my people.

"It seems the scroll originated from somewhere up Mount Incidium."

I don't recognize it. "Where is that at?"

"It's the tallest mountain in Bardus. You can see it from here."

I remember noticing a tall peak in the distance. "What's a scroll written here doing all the way over in Sulamay Island?"

He shrugs. "It's hard to know for certain, but my guess is whoever wrote this scroll visited both places. Maybe even lived there for a while."

"Someone in history lived on both Omanska and Bardus?" It's strange to think of. "I wonder if this person was a human or an elf."

"I don't know as far as this scroll is concerned, but if they left another scroll behind, it would tell us more."

"It's possible there are more scrolls?" If the words of this writer are to be believed, maybe there is hope for something more for my people. What would they say? What more can we do?

"Very. I haven't heard of any like this before, but the writer speaks like they are quite prolific. There's a lot more to the writer's words than I have uncovered. It's very possible that there are more scrolls."

"Up Mount Incidium?"

"Possibly."

"This is something," I say. This is important. If it talked about how my marriage to the human prince could end strife between our countries, what else could it say? It seems like a gem, not just to the history of both our people, but to our future as well. "I wonder..."

"Now don't go getting any ideas that would put you in danger."

I want to laugh—not a normal laugh, but a maniacal, crazed one. "Nowhere is safe for me. I was attacked in this very castle. At my own wedding. Unless I lock myself in a prison and swallow the key, I don't think I'll be safe. Even then, it's questionable."

He gives me a look of pity with his creased faced. "I've heard stories about what you've been through, but it doesn't mean you should go making rash decisions."

"Who's making rash decisions?" Robert asks, striding into the library.

"This girl right here." Andries points a finger at me.

Robert gives me a look.

"I didn't even say what I was thinking. Maybe it's a perfectly sound idea."

"All right, then," Andries says. "What is it?"

"I should go up the mountain to see if I can discover more information about these scrolls."

"That's probably not a good idea," Robert says.

"Why not?"

"There are pirates everywhere. We can't have you taken again."

"But they attacked me here, at the palace. If we could find a way to get out, without them knowing, they'll never look for me up a random mountain."

"Maybe, but what if they do find you? You won't have the protection offered here at the palace."

"Someone could come with me. Besides, I'm good with a sword. If I had one at the wedding, things might have turned out differently."

Robert shakes his head. "You like putting yourself in danger too much."

"I agree," Andries says. "Though you may have a point. I don't think anyone would expect you to go climbing up a mountain right now."

"You agree with her?"

"I'm saying it might happen without the pirates knowing she's gone."

"Last time she tried to out-trick them, she ended up on the run from them."

"Yes," I say, cutting into their argument. "But last time I was left on an island, with no protection and no way to get off. Plus, Octavian told Captain Smythe where I was. That won't happen this time."

Robert lets out a deep sigh. "You'd have to take more than one person. Several guards, I'd think."

"You're considering this?" I ask.

"Just considering. If you do this, I think it would be best that Jocelyn stayed behind. She could help be your decoy."

"I don't like that idea. What if they hurt her instead of me?"

"Circumstances are different this time, as you pointed out. We're different this time. I think it would be wise to leave her, so as to say you're still in the castle but not coming out where everyone can see you. Jocelyn could take food to the rooms as if you were waiting inside."

Stubbornness takes hold of me. "I could take her anyway. I don't need permission to go."

Robert sighs, like he feels the whole weight I've been carrying, and guilt strikes me. I shouldn't be pushing so hard, especially when he's willing to see that maybe I should go, but I can't imagine doing something without her.

"Sorry," I say. "Everything I've done lately has been with her. We've grown into close friends, and it would be hard to leave her."

"It's always hard to leave those you care about." Robert's voice is gruff, like he's holding back some emotion.

I look at him then. *Really* look at him. His golden eyes seem to be saying something to me. About me. I can't look away, but then, neither does he. Time seems to freeze as we watch one another, something passing between us.

Andries clears his throat, and I blush. He says, "I hate to interrupt, but I have work that needs attention. Besides, if the princess is to leave and return before it's time to go to Amara, it should be a swift decision."

From the look on his face, it's not his work that needs attention, but time needed to mourn. But he's right, there's not much time.

Robert runs his fingers through his hair. "I'll go with you if you think it's the right choice."

"I do think it's the right one," I say. "Thank you for your support."

"I'll get some guards and supplies ready to go after I tell the king what's happening. You can tell Jocelyn, but I feel the less people know about this, the better."

"Agreed."

"Do you think you can be ready to leave within the hour?"

"I will be if I hurry." I don't give him a chance to reconsider. I thank Andries and hurry out of the room. It doesn't take long to find Jocelyn and tell her the news. Though she's upset to not be joining me, she understands and helps me prepare for a week-long journey. I hope it doesn't take that long, or it might be pushing it to get back before the boat leaves. Not that it would leave without me, but I can't have everyone waiting for me either.

If all goes well, I'll be not only hidden from those who want to do me harm, but I'll also find out what secrets lie in the past.

Chapter
TWENTY

~

W

E TAKE THE SERVANTS' PASSAGE out of
the castle. We're dressed as servants with my
ears spelled to be rounded. It's easy enough; I'm
not recognizable here as I'd be at my castle. Robert is, though.
There are many greetings to him as we move about, which
should be expected if he's lived here long. He says he's taking
a leisurely stroll, when anyone asks, and then meaningfully
grabs my hand and winks at them. Though I know it's for
show, I blush every time.

Once we're out of the castle, we meet the guards, including
Joseph, and head out of Corona. The city is as I left it before,
only this time I'm seeing pirates everywhere I look. There are
so many people. Any one of them could mean us harm. I'm
grateful when we reach the farms surrounding the city. From
there, it only takes a couple hours to reach the mountainside.

I miss Jocelyn. I didn't realize how much I've come to turn
to her and her friendship. Her chatter is something I could

use on this journey. With Robert and the guards as my only company, it's quiet. Much too quiet.

The guards talk among themselves, but Robert and I remain silent. It's an awkward silence. One that makes me think of our relationship and how it never can be. After the wedding, I won't be able to be friends with him. It will hurt too much. Thinking of it makes me want to go running back to the castle, except we have a job to do. I have to find those scrolls, if they exist.

The walk isn't hard at first. The land slopes upward in a gentle way, trees all around. But as the day goes on, the land becomes steeper and steeper. I silently sing praises when we stop for a break.

"Whew," I say. "I'm not accustomed to this type of climbing."

The guards aren't either—they're out of breath as well—but Robert stands there, like we haven't been hiking at all. I don't know how he does it; looking at him takes my breath away.

"Let's camp here for the night," he says.

"Are we far enough up the mountain?" I ask.

"We've been hiking all day. We should be, but on the safe side, we won't have a fire tonight."

"Sounds wise." I smile, being with him filling me with happiness, even if it's touched with sadness at the thought of losing him again soon.

When he smiles back, a tingle races through me. Is it wrong to be up here with him, like this? What does Abner think of the arrangement? There are guards with us, so it's not as if we're alone, yet it feels intimate. It's the most we've been alone for such a long period of time. There was always some thing or other to call one of us away when we were together before.

The thoughts linger as I help get camp ready for the night. I'm grateful to have learned how to do this by now from all the watching I've done.

"We'll get it," one of the guards says.

"But I can help." I think.

"I know you can"—kindness tinting his words—"but this is one of the few ways we can assist you. Please let us do it."

I stand back, and my eyes sting as I watch five humans prepare camp for the night. I didn't think the day would come when so many humans would not just willingly, but happily, do something for me.

Once they're finished, Robert comes to stand beside me.

"They're good men," I say.

"I chose the best. They're all friendly to elves. I thought that would help."

"It does. Thank you." More than he knows. I can't imagine going on this trip with anyone else. It's wonderful to go on a journey where I'm not running for my life and I'm with those I can trust at my side.

"Tell me," I say. "I've been awful curious about Captain Zaccheus ever since we sailed with him. How is it you and he came to know each other?"

"He's been a family friend for years. I can remember him as well as my own father."

"So he's sort of like Constance was to me?"

"Exactly." He moves so he's standing in front of me, instead of to the side. "I wanted to tell you how sorry I am she died, especially the way she did."

I feel the familiar burn behind my eyes whenever I talk about her. "Thank you. It's been hard without her. I can't help but wonder what she'd think of all this. She'd have insisted on coming with us, at the very least. She'd say we need a proper chaperone, if she let me go at all."

He hesitates a moment and then says, "Maybe she'd be right. Maybe we should have brought a better chaperone than the guards."

I shrug. "Probably. But I think it would have made it harder for us to get away without alerting people. Taking our guards with us seems like too much."

"But we need them, so it was worth it."

"We haven't so far." I wonder what it'd be like to be up here all alone with Robert. I glance at the hard dirt.

"And hopefully it stays that way. But they're here in case."

It's just as well. Being alone with Robert would mean trouble. It feels that way even having the guards here. He stands a proper distance away, but I want to step closer, to lean forward, to let that current flowing between us go wherever it wants to take us.

He seems to sense the change too. He lowers his head and flickers his gaze to my lips. I can't help but follow my instinct to move closer. So close, I can feel the heat coming off him. I look up at him, a warming sensation moving through me.

"We're all done here," a guard says.

Robert and I jump apart. Though there's more distance between us, the tension is still there.

"Good," Robert says, choking up. "Why don't we settle in for the night?"

He looks at me, and all I can do is blush. This is too intimate a setting to be with someone who's not my betrothed. I'd be much more comfortable if Abner was here instead of him. Then again, *comfortable* isn't the right word. More like uptight and stressed. Better than whatever is going on between Robert and me.

I take another step back from Robert and glance over at the guards. Joseph is watching us with an intense gaze. Maybe we do have enough of a chaperone.

Chapter
TWENTY-ONE
❧

T HE NEXT DAY DOESN'T dawn early enough. After a fitful sleep, I'm anxious to be on my feet and moving. I dress myself,—much easier in the peasant clothes Jocelyn helped me pack—have a quick breakfast, and we're on our way for the day.

We climb the mountain until we come to a spot thick with shrubs. One of the guards lifts his sword to hack at it.

"Do we have to destroy it?" I ask, my heart hurting for the plant.

"If we want to get through it, we do." He grimaces, though, as if he feels guilty for telling me so.

"Can we keep damage to a minimum?"

As the guard hacks through it, Robert joins me. "Are you doing all right with all this walking?"

"I'm better prepared than I was last time we went on a long hike together."

"Really? How are you better prepared?"

"I've been exercising more. Not just working on my sword-fighting skills, but trying to keep my entire body in shape for long distances. I don't want to be caught in that situation again."

"Me neither."

I wince as a big chunk of plant is cut.

"Are plants really that special to you?" Robert asks.

I nod. "It would be nice if you could feel it. Plants are living, like we are. I've felt it more times than I can count while helping them with my magic."

"I can't imagine what that's like."

"I wish there was a way to show you."

He looks at me, and I can't help the heat that rises to my cheeks. There are a lot of things I want to show him. Things I want him to show me. Mostly though, I wish his best friend wasn't the one standing between us. He and duty. Duty is the biggest culprit. If I didn't care so much about my people, things could be different.

Once we get through the thick spot of shrubs, we search for a place that might fit a cave the likes a person could live in. My mind is full of thoughts of who this scroll came from. Why would one be on Sulamay Island, with more on Bardus? It's a long way to travel when humans and elves have been divided for so long.

Was it someone like Andries, who does what he wants and ignores the anger of others? Or was there some other reason for them living in more than one place? I hope when we find the scrolls they'll not only hold answers to our history, but also clues to who this person was. *If* we find them.

It takes two more days of hiking and searching before I start to worry we'll never find anything.

"What exactly are we looking for?" a guard asks.

"I don't know. Some place that a person could hide in, like a cave." I keep looking, hoping something will pop up before the day's end. It has to be here somewhere. It just has to.

We move through the top of the mountain more slowly, combing every inch. There are a couple caves, but they're empty of anything except a few critters. We hike up and down, hunting for something that could be home to the scrolls I so desperately want to find, but nothing.

"If we don't find something quickly, we'll have to go back," Robert says.

"There's still time," I reply.

"Not much. If we don't leave soon, we won't have enough food for the way back. We can scrounge, but the others will be worried about us."

"Plus we have to be back for the boat." I sigh, wishing I could stay out in the wilderness with Robert for the rest of my life. It's much preferable to being chased by pirates. But there are friends and family I'd miss. Not to mention a country of people who need me. Make that two. The humans need me, whether they think they do or not.

Sunset is coming. Soon we'll have to give up for the day, though I'm not ready to be done. If we don't find it now, we never will. We'll have to start heading back, and while we can look on our way there, there's too much ground to cover. Too many places a cave could be hiding in. It was a long shot coming out here, anyway.

Still, I keep looking. I can't give up when it could be so close. No matter how hard I tell myself that, though, I can feel myself giving up. We don't have enough time and people.

Maybe after I'm married, when things have calmed down, I'll be able to come back with more people and search the mountain better. Until then, I'll have to be content with the fact that we tried.

"I think I've found something," Robert says.

My spirits rise. Something inside me springs to life. I move toward Robert, not seeing anything at first. He stands at the side of a mountain, tackling a bush and trying to move it away from the mountainside. Only, it isn't a mountainside but a narrow mouth to a cave.

As soon as Robert clears the opening, I hurry closer.

"Let me go first," he says. "Make certain there's nothing dangerous in there."

That makes me take a step back. "Please."

I grab the hilt of my sword in case something comes flying out, but nothing does. He comes out a moment later. "It's clear, but we need to light a torch. I can't see much."

The guards hurry to put a couple of torches together. Once they're ready, Robert says to me, "Lead the way."

Excitement races through me. This is it. I know it is. I can feel it deep inside me. I enter the cave, Robert close behind.

It's smaller than I expected, but still big enough for someone to live in—and live in it someone did. It's difficult to tell how long ago the space was used, but it must have been hundreds of years ago. Layers of dirt and grime cover every-thing. Creatures have made their homes here. It's musty and smells of animal, and yet, there's evidence of a life lived. A bed, just big enough for two, rotted through now.

I swat away the dust coming down from the ceiling as I continue to explore the space. Shelves are set against one wall, above a table. It's full of spoons and vases. A cradle in one corner.

I slap again at all the dust falling, and then I realize it's not dust. It's baby spiders. I run from the cave with a squeal, swatting at my hair and clothes to get rid of the spiders that probably tried to make a home of me.

Robert comes out of the cave and watches with keen interest as I make a fool of myself. "Is everything all right?" he asks.

"No." I don't stop my frantic cleaning. "All that dust?"

"What about it?"

"Baby spiders."

Robert grunts and begins shaking himself off. As I calm down, I watch him do a crazy sort of dance to get rid of all the spiders. I can't help but laugh, thinking how I must have looked a moment ago.

The guards join in, and Robert glares at them. "You're welcome to go in and search for the scroll," he says.

That quiets them, but I laugh harder. "You should see the look on all of your faces. I think pirates are less terrifying then spiders."

My guards look sheepish but don't disagree, which makes me giggle more. After another moment, I settle down. "We should go back in there," I say.

Robert shudders. "I don't think I want to."

"I don't love the idea, but I'm all right with going back in," I say.

"What if they're poisonous?"

"Then we'd already be bitten."

"I don't like this."

"We can't have come all this way and not find out if there are more scrolls. It would be a waste of time and resources."

"Fine. But be careful."

I grin. "If I scream, will you come in and save me?"

"Only if you scream."

I giggle, and then somber as I realize I'm going back into a spider-infested cave. Disgusting. I head to the cave's opening and walk through. Instead of holding my torch like normal, I reach it above my head to touch the ceiling above, hoping it will kill the tiny spiders before they land on me. Oh, please, let it kill any spiders. I don't want any more of those nasty things on me.

I creep into the cave. The room is much as I left it before, only creepier now I know there are thousands of spiders trying to crawl on me. No sense dawdling when that's the case.

I go to the first place I'm likely to find the scrolls—the vases on the shelves above the table. The first I open is empty, as is the second. The third doesn't have a lid on it, so I peek inside. Nothing. Same with the rest of them. They're all empty, as are the areas under the table and bed.

Where could they be? With all this time and weather, maybe they're gone. Or maybe someone found them and took them long before I came along. Or maybe they were never here to begin with. Though this place doesn't look like it's been disturbed in a long time, that could still be the case. Maybe one hundred years ago someone had the same idea as me or got curious.

This is a hopeless task. What was I thinking, coming all the way up here? I should have stayed down in the valley and taken the pirates and naysayers head on. Instead, I ran up the mountain on a fruitless task. What next?

"Is everything all right in there?" Robert calls.

"I haven't been bitten by a spider yet, if that's what you mean."

"Let's keep it that way."

I should hurry. Feeling defeated, I consider a cradle in the corner. Whoever lived here before had a baby. It matches the writing on the scroll, which makes me believe the rest of it could be true too. I glance inside, but there's nothing but old wood. That may be all it is now, but some day it meant a lot more to a mother and father.

I step away to go when I realize I didn't look under the cradle. Not that anything would be there, but I check anyway. There's a pottery of some sort. I reach for it, my chest warming with hope.

A large spider drops onto my hand. I give a little shriek and jump to shake it off. Robert comes running in.

"Don't worry," I say. "I think I found the mommy spider."

He shudders. "Did you find anything else?"

"There's a vase or something under this cradle. I'm hoping it has something. Otherwise, this place is a loss."

"Do you want me to look under there?"

Yes. "It's fine. Just don't be surprised if I scream again. I don't know where momma spider went." And unfortunately, I can't put the torch under the cradle or I'd set it on fire.

I take a deep breath, hold it, and reach under the cradle. I hurry to grab the pottery and run toward the exit. "We can look at this outside."

"Good." Robert runs after me. "I don't want to spend any more time in here."

We come crashing out of the cave to find the guards watching us with amused expressions. I don't care at this point. I carefully put the pottery down and hand my torch to one of them, then swat at myself like a mad woman, trying to rid myself of any pests that may have come out with me. My only consolation is Robert does the same. We must look like a couple of crazies. At least the sun is going down so that it's harder to see what we're doing.

"I hope I got them all," I say.

"Better have. Spiders are nasty." He scowls.

"Now I know how to get whatever I want from you," I say with a grin. "Threaten you with spiders."

"You only have to ask to get what you want from me." His voice goes serious and low.

My cheeks heat as my heart misses a beat. The problem is I can't ask for what I really want. Him.

I clear my throat and turn toward the pottery that's now on the ground. "Do you think it's in there?"

"Only one way to find out." He moves to stand next to it.

The lid shakes from my trembling as I open it. It's too dark to see inside, and I'm not anxious to put my hand in there blindly. I could plop it over upside down, but I don't want to damage the scrolls if they are in there. I turn toward the guards. "Would one of you please bring a torch over so we can see if there's anything in here?"

Joseph steps forward, his movements seemingly slow, though he walks at a normal pace. I bite my lip to keep from asking him to move faster. He gets to us and lifts his torch near the pot. I look inside.

Something is in here. Something that looks a lot like a scroll. Now I know there's not another bug waiting for me, I reach in and pull it out.

It *is* a scroll, much like the one we found on Sulamay Island. Andries was right. Something more was left behind. I want to open it and read it, but it's already cracked in places, so I don't dare.

I carefully put it back in the vase and smile. *This is it.* This is what we came looking for.

Robert grins at me, and it takes everything in me not to hug him. He says, "We've done it."

Chapter
TWENTY-TWO

W E SHOULD HEAD BACK DOWN and get this to Andries," I say, yet part of me is hesitant to get back to the real world.

"We should," Robert says, though the tone of his voice sounds as dejected as I feel.

"Let's get going, then," Joseph says and moves to grab our packs.

I want to tell him to stop. To wait. But we can't. We've been gone almost a week already—enough time that the pirates might have realized we tricked them into thinking I never left. We don't want to worry anyone by being gone too long. I'm not ready to leave the quiet peace I've found with Robert up here, though. Even with the guards, it's more than I've been able to find before.

When neither Robert nor I move, the guards look to us.

"Is there something else we need to do?" Joseph asks.

"No," Robert replies. "No, there isn't."

But there's a loss I'll have, not being up here with him anymore. It feels like cheating on Abner, but him and I don't have a love connection. Besides, we're not married yet, and Robert and I have done nothing wrong, though I want to. I ache to lean into him. To put my hands on his shoulders. To rest my head against his chest. To hear his heart beating in time with mine.

What's more, I long to stretch up to my full height and touch my lips to his. To feel what it's like to kiss and be kissed. By him. He's what I want—what I yearn for. No one else makes me feel the way he does. I can't imagine how good it would feel to brush my lips against his.

To be with him and only him. To give him my heart. My love.

I can't think of anything greater.

But we can't.

Not now. Not ever. Not when I'm to marry his best friend, the prince of Bardus.

Chapter
TWENTY-THREE

⌒

THE JOURNEY DOWN THE MOUNTAIN goes faster now we're not searching for something. Every step takes us closer to the palace and farther from the bit of freedom we found here. If only I wasn't a princess.

But then, I would have never met Robert in the first place.

I try not to dwell on it too much, but with just him and the guards around, it's difficult to think of anything else. I consider reading the scroll, but I'm afraid of breaking their fragile state.

After four days' journey down the mountain, I'm tired and aching, but happy we found what we were looking for and for spending time with Robert. I'm not ready to return to Corona, though, and I'm definitely not ready to return home and to my wedding. The thought of my upcoming nuptials dampens my mood. Why is it I have to go through this twice, each time with Robert at my side, making me fall harder for him?

"Look what we have here," a familiar male voice says.

I glance up from my daydreaming to find Aiden striding toward us. My guards draw their swords as several pirates come out of the forest on both sides of him. I want to take a step back, but I force myself to stand my ground. I have as many guards as he has pirates. Besides, I know his powers now and know better than to get close to him. Plus, I have my sword. Many things going for me. Not many going for him. I hope.

"I'd recommend you move on," Robert says.

"It's Aiden," I whisper.

He nods. "Figured as much."

"I'm not going anywhere," Aiden says. "Not without the princess."

"Like I'd go with you after what happened last time. I wouldn't be caught dead doing anything with you willingly."

He frowns. "I was hoping you'd be more cooperative than that."

"You're not very bright, are you?"

His scowl deepens. "You're the one goading the elf with all the power around here. If anyone is dimwitted, it's you."

His insult has no effect on me. I've dealt with much worse from people I actually care about.

"Captain Smythe has a place waiting for you," he says. "It's time to go."

My guards and Robert step closer to me.

"She's not going anywhere with you," Robert says.

"Then I guess we'll have to figure this out the old-fashioned way."

Aiden takes a step toward me. My guards surround me completely. He laughs and motions for his fellow pirates to move forward. That's all it takes before battle cries and clanging reverberate.

Though I'm safe behind my guards for now, I draw my sword. In no time at all, my guards are fighting for their lives. The clash of swords hitting each other fills the air. A gap opens up in the area around me and a pirate dives for it.

I meet him head on with my sword. He parries the move and swivels his blade around mine to try to cut my shoulder. I guess Captain Smythe no longer cares what condition I'm in. That makes the fight all the more dangerous.

I knock the pirate's sword aside. With a quick thrust of my sword, I aim for his stomach. He blocks me. As the fight continues, sweat beads on my forehead. The ground beneath me is firm, giving me a good place to push off from, but that gives him the same advantage.

One of my guards knocks him on the side of the head. He backs up, leaving my guards to close the gap again.

I'm heaving for air from the exertion. It can't have been much time, but it felt like too long. These pirates are skilled. I glance at my guards to find they're barely holding their own. Something has to change here if we hope to not just survive, but escape.

Someone grabs my hair and yanks. I start to fall backward but catch myself. I twist around to find another pirate has broken through my pack of guards. He moves his grip from my hair to my upper arm. I bring my sword around toward his wrist.

He lets go, sending me falling backward. This time I don't stop myself, instead landing on the dirt with a hard *thump*.

He reaches for me. Not happening. I sweep my sword toward him, and he darts back.

"Come on, wench," he growls.

I ignore his words and jump to my feet. Robert is fighting as fiercely as I want to be. So far none of my guards appear to be hurt, but it's only a matter of time. I take them all in and find myself coming back to the pirate taunting me.

He points his sword at me and reaches forward like he's going to grab my wrist. I dart it back and attack. I throw everything I have into it. Our fierce fight fills the forest air with its cacophony.

"Give up," he says.

"Never."

I keep him at bay, but barely. A guard turns to help me. Someone calls out in pain. I can't tell if it's someone on my side or the pirates'.

I can't think about it now. If one of my men is injured, I'll tend to him afterward. There isn't time now. My guard continues to help me until a second pirate joins the fray and forces him away from me.

I thrust my sword forward before slamming it as hard as I can into the pirate's sword. He falls back under my blow, but quickly recovers. I don't have the strength required to face him head on like I want. I have to go around him. Be quicker than he is. I swirl my sword around and cut his forearm. He jumps back.

My guards once again fill the gap, but it's hard for them. We're losing, unless something changes fast.

Aiden doesn't want me to use magic against them, so that's what I'm going to do. I call on my power and bring it forward. I think of that spell I used before—the one that shocked the pirates. If there's a way to do that on a small scale, without touching anyone, it'll be helpful.

I should have practiced once I realized I could do something different. I've had all this time running from the pirates and wandering up the mountain, and it could have made a difference.

Focusing on the closest pirate, I try to replicate that feeling and shoot it across to him. Though I feel a little tingling, nothing else happens, and then one of the pirates breaks through the line so there isn't more time to try. I must defeat him.

Our swords meet in a clash, and I have an idea. I send the tingling that's in me through my sword. As soon as the blades meet again, I push the tingling from my sword down through his. That does the trick. He jolts away as if my sword had cut into him.

He doesn't stop but backs away from me until one of my guards butts him on the head with the hilt of his sword and knocks him to the ground.

One down, but more to go.

Robert blocks an attacker coming at me, but there are more and more. It seems like they are trying to reach me and don't care about the others. A mistake on their part, but there's no more time to consider it. As I parry and thrust my sword, I think of that electric feeling I just felt. If I can do that more, perhaps they'll be scared enough to run away. Elves are scary with their magic, after all.

I call on the electric current, run it down my sword, and thrust it at whatever comes my way. Several more pirates go down before they become more wary of me.

Aiden comes at me like he's not afraid. It strikes me that if I can do this with my magic, he might be able to counteract it. Better not to find out. I have to beat him.

Our swords clang, and I quickly pull away, dodging and evading while I call on my magic. It's tired. Lethargic. I feel it deep within my bones. I don't know how much longer I'll be able to go on without falling asleep.

One more minute—that's all I need. If I can manage this without touching him, it might just work. Robert is at my side, helping me evade Aiden. But Aiden is determined. He comes at me, face scrunched up with determination.

I send my magic in a giant wave, the biggest I can manage, straight through my sword. I purposefully hit my blade against his, so the magic continues down his sword and to him.

As soon as it hits him, he jumps away and lands on the ground a few feet from me, knocked out. At his defeat, the other pirates tuck tail and run. Thankfully, because I can feel myself going.

"Sleep," I tell Robert. "I'm going to sleep for a week."

"Me, too, I think."

"No, really." My words slur together. "Cost of magic. Sleep."

And the world goes black.

Chapter
TWENTY-FOUR

❧

EVERYTHING IS FOGGY. Every bone in my body aches. I feel as if I've been pulled apart and stomped back together. The world sways, but not like a boat. It's in an uneven, bumpy sort of sway. I open my eyes to find the sky littered with tree tops, the top half of a guard, and Robert—all moving.

"She's awake," Robert says, looking down at me.

They set what I realize is some sort of carrier on the ground. It's uneven and hard beneath me.

"How long have I been out?" I ask.

"Three days," Joseph says from where he stands by my feet.

"Three long days," Robert says.

No wonder my stomach feels like it's trying to eat itself. It's better than the week it took last time, though. "Was anyone hurt or…" I hate to say it, but it needs to be said. "Or killed?"

"No one was killed."

"But…?"

"There are some injuries. Nothing too serious, but they'll take a while to heal."

"I'm sorry there were injuries because of me."

"It was our duty," one of the guards answers. "And we were happy to do it."

"Thank you." The world continues to waver around me. "Have you been carrying me the whole time?"

Robert kneels at my side. "No. We waited a day, and then we decided we better get moving if we were to make it home before everyone started to worry and we ran out of supplies."

So we've been traveling for two days. We're that much closer to the castle and my destiny. I try to sit up, but it doesn't work. I fall back toward the ground, but Robert catches me. He puts an arm on my back and a hand on my upper arm and guides me up, leaving his arms in place once I'm sitting. A thrill goes through me at being touched by him. At being so near him.

"Take it slow," he says. "We can keep carrying you for a while. All the way to the castle, if we need to."

"I hope it doesn't take that long to regain my feet." I wish I could jump up and walk right now, but I'm having a hard time sitting up, even with Robert's help. "What happened to the pirates and Aiden?"

"Aiden was out cold, or so we thought. We were attending you when he woke up and ran off," Robert says.

"We tried to chase them," Joseph says, "but they were gone faster than we could get to them."

"Drat," I say. "Not that it would do much good. We don't have the means to take them with us, and we know they won't talk."

"But it would be nice if they did talk to us," Robert says. "We need a break from them."

"More than a break," I say. "We need to get downright lucky for a long period of time. I'm starting to lose hope that we'll be able to capture Captain Smythe."

"Don't say that. There's always hope."

I sigh. "I know. It's a lot harder than I thought it would be. I never could have guessed it was so hard to capture his crew, let alone him."

"We'll get him. One of these days he'll mess up, and we'll have him."

I'm tired of thinking about it. "How close are we to Corona?"

"We're almost there. We should reach it by nightfall."

"Can you help me stand?"

"Are you sure you should be on your feet?" Concern laces his words.

"I'm beginning to feel okay. I think I needed some time to recover from using up my magic. Let's see if I can walk with you." I'd rather be on my own two feet when we return, than carried in like an invalid. Besides, staring up at Robert the entire time isn't helpful to my sanity.

As I try to stand, Robert helps lift me by the arm. I stumble to my feet and crash into him. It feels good, despite my weakness. To feel his chest heave against mine. To feel his hand linger at my waist.

But there are guards about, and I'm promised to another.

I pull away, though slowly and with much regret. My legs seem steady enough. I stretch and ease the last of the sleepy heaviness from my body. "I think I can walk for a while. I'm feeling pretty good. Do we have anything to drink and eat? I'm starving."

Joseph pulls out a biscuit and some water for me, which I quickly do away with. He hands me another biscuit, and I nibble on it as we walk.

Despite the way I started the day, it's rather lovely out— warm, but with a cool breeze lingering that brings a fresh scent to the air. Birds are singing their musical way. If it weren't for pirates and a pending marriage, I'd think it a most glorious day. Especially for the company.

I sneak a peek at Robert to find him peeking back at me. A blush heats my cheeks.

"Are you sure you don't need to be carried?" he asks as we continue on.

"I'm fine. I'm doing better all the time." Feeling brave, I say back. "What about you? Do you need to be carried into Corona?"

He gives a chuckle. "Not today."

"Hopefully not any day."

"I'm sure we could carry you if we needed to," Joseph says, startling me back to the fact that the guards are with us.

"And I could carry you," Robert replies, "if the need should arise."

Joseph winks at me in a good-natured way and turns his attention ahead. The other five guards are behind Robert and me. They've protected me like this the whole trip, even when there wasn't any danger. But the danger is real now. I'm grateful for their presence and their willingness to help me—an elf. Why are they willing to help me?

"I want to thank you all for coming on this trip with us," I say. "I don't know what we would have done without you."

"It was my pleasure," the guard next to Joseph says. "I'd do it again any day. This was much more exciting than our usual duties."

"Is that why you came?" I ask. "For some excitement?"

"Maybe. As nice as it is to get a break from the tedium of everyday duties, it's nice to help too."

"And we don't have to wear a uniform," a guard behind me says.

I laugh. "That's definitely a benefit." If they hate wearing their uniforms half as much as I hate having to be dolled up, then it's a benefit indeed.

We hike down the mountain the rest of the day. Sometimes we talk, and sometimes we don't, but either way I can't help but feel like I'm about to leave friends behind. Especially Robert. How can I think of him as just a friend, though? The longer I'm with him, the more he means to me. How am I ever going to have an honest marriage with his best friend?

Chapter
TWENTY-FIVE

W HEN WE GET TO THE BOTTOM of the mountain, we sneak in the castle, and I go straight to Andries, everyone insisting on going with me. I find him in the library, like he hasn't moved the entire time I've been gone.

"We found them," I say.

"You're safe," he says, rushing to my side. "We've been most worried about you."

"Yes, yes, I'm fine. We all are. But please look these over." I hand him the scroll. "I haven't been able to make out anything, and I was afraid of handling them too much because of breaking them."

"You were wise to wait to bring them to me," he says. He slowly unrolls the parchment, taking great care not to tear it.

The script is hard to read, parts completely blocked out, but there are two words that are familiar to me.

"Pomum Heart," I say. "That's in Omanska."

"Let's see what we can find there." He takes out a brush and gently brushes away some of the dirt. He switches tools and continues to work. I hover over his shoulder, anxious for any progress. The first part becomes clear.

> *Pomum Heart was my favorite place to dwell. Not anymore. I hoped it would be a place of peace, had greed not taken over the people. The stones are torn asunder and stolen from that most scared of places.*

"What does it mean, about the stones? Why mention those?" I ask.

"It's hard to know, without uncovering more," Andries murmurs, more lost in his work than focused on anything I have to say.

I continue to watch as he works, and a little more becomes apparent.

> *The memories fill me as I sing softly to my little one. Memories of hiding from the humans as well as the elves. I fear both want me dead. My people. Had they known me better, they would realize all I want for them as their princess is to love one another and treat each other with kindness.*
>
> *Instead, screams fill the air as I hide the scrolls.*

"More scrolls?" I ask. "Do you think we can find them in Pomum Heart?"

"I hope we can. I'm certain these seem to dwell with an elf with the power of sight. Maybe she has more information about your marriage and the healing of our two races."

And that elf with the power of sight was a princess like me. I wonder why both the humans and elves wanted her dead.

"Does it say anything about where the scrolls are hidden?"

"It will probably take me a while to look through it. Why don't you let everyone know you're safe and get settled? I will send for you the moment I know anything."

Feeling slightly deflated, but not wanting to show it, I give my agreement. The guards leave to inform the king and queen we've made it back safely, leaving Robert and me alone in a hall. There's an awkward tension between us that wasn't there before. It's different than when we were hiking up the mountain. More final.

"Let me escort you to your rooms," he says, breaking the silence.

"You don't have to."

"I insist."

Secretly, I'm grateful for the extra time with him but immediately feel guilty for such thoughts. Soon I'll be wed to his best friend, and that will be the end of any thoughts I have about him. I have to stop them now, before the wedding takes place. I might not like Abner much, but that doesn't mean he doesn't deserve my respect.

The walk to the room I'm staying in is too quiet and too quick.

"Thank you," I say when we get there. "I appreciate all that you've done in coming with me."

"I can assure you it was my pleasure."

"But it's over now." My voice wavers.

The look in his eyes says he thinks it's as unfortunate as I do. And now I have to say goodbye to him.

"I guess this is goodbye." I hope he understands I mean for good, though we're certain to see more of each other.

"I guess it is." But he doesn't move. Doesn't take his gaze off of me. "Arabella, I want you to know something."

"What is that?" I feel breathless.

He opens his mouth, and then closes it again. With a shake of his head, he says, "It was good being able to find that lost scroll with you."

I lean in closer, though I shouldn't. That's not what he was going to say. I don't know what it was, but I think I would have liked to hear it. "It was good. I'll cherish the memories, as distant as they may become."

"I will as well."

With one last look, he turns and walks away.

Chapter
TWENTY-SIX

⟅⟆

THE THRONE ROOM is silent as I make my way
to the king, queen, and prince. Robert is nowhere in
sight. I won't be surprised if he's already spoken to
them. I stop and give a curtsy. The king and queen both nod
at me. I wonder why Belle isn't here, and if she's still busy preparing for her mother's birthday.

"Come closer, child," the king says.

I'm not much of a child anymore, especially not after these
long months. Still, to him I suppose I'm more a child than
not, so I don't take offense. I make my way right up next to
the thrones.

"What have you learned?" the queen asks.

Perhaps Robert hasn't been here as of yet. "Not much so
far, but I'm hopeful we'll learn a lot. We recovered a scroll.
Andries is already in the process of restoring them as we
speak. He seems confident he'll be able to do so."

"And you're safe," Abner says, surprising me.

"Yes. We had a little incident, but nothing more, though we do have guards out scouring the city for any remaining pirates. I feel it was a successful rouse."

"There was an incident here as well. They thought you were still in the palace until recently."

Worry pounds through me. I couldn't forgive myself if someone else was hurt on my account. "Is everyone well?"

"Well enough," the king replies. "There were a few injuries, but they're minor."

"And what of Jocelyn? I haven't seen her since I arrived."

"She's well," Abner replies. "Her room was moved after the incident. We we'll moving you into a chamber next to hers. It's an inside room, so not as elegant, but it should be safer, as long as the pirates don't make it into the castle."

I didn't expect Abner to be the one to know where Jocelyn is. I'm surprised he remembers her at all. A little something must have changed since I left. Though it wasn't long, I feel changed too. Heavier. More world worn.

The door behind me opens. I glance back to find Robert striding toward us.

He kneels before the king and queen and then comes to stand next to me. "It was a successful mission." He makes it sound so impersonal. To me, it was anything but. I feel flustered just thinking about it, but there's no reason for it. Everything was kept proper.

"Thank you, Robert," the king says. "That will be all."

I expect him to turn and leave, but instead he goes and stands beside Abner. His gaze bores into me. I try not to look at him, but it's difficult. It takes all my attention to keep focused on the royal couple.

"Now," the king says, "I think it's time we head back to Amara, to see this wedding finally happen. Your parents are most anxious to see you."

This perks me up. "Have they sent word? They know I'm well and safe?"

"They have, and they do. They hope you can return home as soon as possible. We will journey with you, so the wedding can take place without further delay."

Now I feel both Robert's and Abner's gazes boring into me, but I don't glance at either of them. I don't know how I feel, let alone want to share my feelings with others.

"I believe that would be most wise. How soon can we leave?" I ask.

"We can be ready tomorrow if that works for you."

So soon? I give the best smile I can manage. "Tomorrow, it is."

Chapter
TWENTY-SEVEN

༄

I'M HELPING JOCELYN pack the last few of our things that the queen provided us with when there's a knock on the door. Jocelyn moves to answer it.

"Is Princess Arabella here?" a male voice says.

"I can give her a message." Very good response from Jocelyn.

"Would you take this to her?"

"I would. Good day to you." She starts to close the door.

"I will wait here for a reply." His reply sounds through the wood.

Now I'm curious. Jocelyn brings the note to me. "It was an elf."

"Oh?" This adds to my curiosity. I unwrap the note.

My dearest Arabella,

We are overcome with relief to hear you have been found safely. Please know we love and cherish you. We have sent a gift for you with the messenger. We hope to see you soon.

Yours,

 —Mother and Father

The royal seal follows. I clutch the note to my chest. A note from my parents written by one of their scribes. I didn't realize how much I missed them until I read this. What must they have been thinking this entire time? They must have been so worried.

"It's from my parents," I tell Jocelyn. "They sent a gift. I'll go see what it is while you finish packing."

"We're about done, anyway. If you don't mind, I'd like to join you."

"Of course."

She opens the door, and we find the elf who delivered the message waiting for us. He gives me a bow. "Your Highness. If you will just accompany me."

We follow him through the halls making several turns and going deeper and deeper into the castle's bowels. It reminds me of when we were sneaking out, to go up the mountain.

It seems strange to have something all the way down here. Could it be a trap from the pirates? No, it couldn't. It had the royal seal on it. I wonder what they've sent that needed to be left down here. Perhaps my horse? My sword is what I really want, though the borrowed one I keep at my side does the job well enough.

"It's just through here." The servant opens a door for us and keeps behind it as we walk through into the darkened room. Something seems off here.

As soon as I cross the threshold, a chill warns me. I take a step back, but it's too late. The door is already closed behind me, and a familiar laugh fills the room.

"You didn't think you'd really escaped me, did you?" Octavian asks.

I stare at him, his bulky frame thinner from his ordeal. He's wearing simple clothes, no rings on his fingers. It makes him almost seem like a new man, except for the cold, calculating look in his eyes. That hasn't changed at all.

"How did you get in here? There's no way around all those guards," I say.

"The same way I got an elf to help me deliver a message. Money talks. Not only that, but I'm not the only one who doesn't want to see you get married to a human."

I'm not surprised by the existence of traitors, but that doesn't make it easier to deal with. I have to figure out a way out of this situation and not dwell on it, though. "I could scream."

"You could, but it wouldn't do any good. Didn't you realize how far away from everyone else you were taken? Or was your excitement over the gift from your parents too great?"

I didn't pay enough attention, other than to think it was quite some distance. And now, here I am, stuck in a bad position with Jocelyn. Again.

"Don't think that you can get away from me and win, like you did before," he says. "Jeshua here is a very powerful elf.

Plus, we're inside, where it's harder to use your nature magic. You may as well give up now."

I glance at him, where he stands across the room from me, and then at Jeshua, close to the door. Might as well risk it. I will not go down without a fight. I draw my sword. I'll even use that power I have to knock them out if needed. Who cares if I'll be out for a week?

I swear Octavian grows paler, but his words defy that expression. "I wouldn't do that if I were you."

I grab Jocelyn and shove her behind me in the opposite corner from Jeshua and Octavian. "You can't stop me. There's nothing you can do to recapture me. I'm marrying the human prince. Leave now, before I gut you."

"Tough words for such a tiny girl."

Lightning fast, I dart toward him, thrust my sword toward his arm and give it a good slash, before returning to my defensive position in front of Jocelyn.

Octavian grabs his bleeding arm. "How dare you?"

"That was a warning. Leave now before I make things worse."

Despite how pale he looks, he laughs. "Oh, things are about to get worse."

I swing my sword to point from him to Jeshua and back again. "It seems we're at an impasse."

The door opens and in walks Aiden followed by Joseph.

"*Joseph*. You have to help us." Though why is he with Aiden?

"I'm not sure I can help you like you want."

Unease flickers through me. "What's going on?"

"I'm sorry, Arabella," Joseph says, "but I have to go with my gut. I know they won't hurt you as long as you do what they say."

I shake my head in disbelief. "Why would you do this?"

"You're a nice enough girl, but I still don't believe humans and elves should mix."

My heart feels as if it's been ripped from me. I keep my sword pointed out at everyone, unsure how to get out of this situation. My shocking power will have to come to the rescue. I only hope it's reliable. "I can't believe you. I thought you were a friend."

"I am. Just one who thinks you shouldn't marry our prince."

"So you what? Listen to Octavian? An elf?"

"Like I said, I have no problem with elves. I don't want our races mixing. Put the sword down, Arabella, and we'll make sure you and Jocelyn make it out of this safe, once we're certain you won't marry the human prince."

"And you agreed to help them?" I turn my gaze to Aiden.

"I know where my loyalty lies."

That answer is more confusing than ever. "And you." I point my sword at Octavian. "What do you hope to gain from this? As soon as they find you, you'll be killed. That's the punishment for breaking a banishment."

"You let me worry about that."

"Whatever your plans are"—I swing my sword at all of them—"you have to have me, and I won't allow it."

"You don't have a choice," Octavian says.

"There's always a choice."

Joseph pulls his sword. "Please don't make me fight you."

"I could say the same to you. I don't want to injure you if I don't have to." Though doubt is filling me. They outnumber me, and I have Jocelyn to protect.

"Hand us your sword," Aiden says. "Between where we are and my powers, your magic will be no use. There are enough of us here. Your sword will only end up injuring someone."

"If you can touch me." Which I won't allow. I can't.

Enough chatter. I thrust my blade toward Joseph's hands to disarm him. He parries, knocking my sword to the side with so much force, I almost lose hold of it. I tighten my grip and strike again. He blocks.

I go at him again, this time faking to his left, whipping my sword in a circle under his, and making contact with his stomach.

My heart sinks as I slide my blade back out. "I never wanted to hurt you."

He touches his injury, and his hand comes away red.

"If you help me instead of fighting me," I say, "I can heal you."

"There's more at stake than a flesh wound."

"Why?" I practically yell. "Why can none of you accept humans and elves can be together? Can work together? As a team, we could make things so much better than they are now. Don't you understand?"

Joseph slashes his sword at me. I block and maneuver a step over to miss his second attack. There's nowhere left to go if I want to protect Jocelyn. If only we could make it to the door, we would have a chance. But too many people are blocking it. There's no hope against so many.

I could give Joseph a shock, but he's not the real danger right now, Aiden is. I need to shock him with my sword again without touching him with my skin.

Next thing I know, Joseph's sword whips past me and stays there at neck level. I ease away to find it pressed against Jocelyn's neck. I curse myself for getting distracted.

"No," I cry out. "Leave her alone."

Octavian gives a slow clap. "Well done, Joseph. You know, I found out about Joseph's loyalties just recently. Word about him complaining in a bar that, as much as he liked you, he couldn't stand the thought of you marrying the prince. I had to take advantage of that. Someone who's gotten close to you. Someone who wants the same thing as I do. For you not to marry the prince."

I clench my jaw, unable to form words at how upset I am over the betrayal.

"Hand over your sword Arabella, and we'll think about not hurting Jocelyn. Maybe."

"You'll think about it? No. I want assurances that you won't hurt her." Not that they can't break their word; it doesn't seem to mean much to them. But how else am I suppose to protect Jocelyn? "I'll do what you want. Just don't hurt her."

"Exactly what we need," Aiden says.

"We should have her write a note," Octavian says.

"No," Aiden replies. "The king and queen will never believe it with all that's been going on with the pirates. We need her to do it in person."

"How can we trust that she'll do what we want?"

"Because she values Jocelyn's life too much not to."

I clench my hand into a fist. He's right. I do value Jocelyn's life, but I also have a whole nation of people to watch out for. Two nations, actually. How am I going to protect both?

"You will go with Joseph and inform the king and queen you no longer wish to marry their son," Aiden says. "You will tell them you'll make your own way home, and then you will return here, to us."

I hang my head. There has to be a way around this. Something that I can do. And I think there is, but it's dangerous. If they catch on to what I'm going to try to, something could happen to Jocelyn. Can I take that risk? "Fine. But you have to promise not to hurt her while I'm gone."

Memories of her being tortured at Captain Smythe's orders still haunt me. I can't have more hurt added to that list.

Joseph grabs me by the wrist and yanks me away from her. Aiden takes his place next to her and puts a dagger to her throat.

"Go on now," he says. "We'll be anxiously awaiting your return with no promises. Not unless you do exactly as I say."

Joseph drags me from the room, and I want to kick him. But I don't dare do anything to jeopardize Jocelyn's safety. I just have to hope I can follow through on my plan. The elf servant takes the opportunity to leave the room and run the opposite way.

All through the winding way, I feel as if I'm in a nightmare. How can this be happening? What if my plan fails? What if Jocelyn dies while I'm trying to save her? It's clear I can't give into what they want, but I can't have anything bad happen to her either.

Fear crawls through me more and more the further we walk. I pay more attention this time, and it takes forever. The halls are bare of people. Bare of any assistance. There's no way I can protect Jocelyn from here. I couldn't even protect her when I was next to her.

We begin to pass other people. I want to call out to them. To beg for help. But they're not the people I need to help me. If I come back with forces enough to stop them, they could kill Jocelyn before we get the chance. I need someone I trust. Someone that can help without costing Jocelyn's life. Joseph and I continue on, each step heavier with dread.

I see Robert and Abner coming toward us. Perfect.

"Is everything all right?" Robert asks, giving me the eye where Joseph still holds my wrist tight.

Joseph lets go and says, "Everything is fine. Princess Arabella has requested an audience with the king and queen, and I'm escorting her to them."

While Joseph talks, Robert doesn't take his gaze from mine. I give a subtle shake of my head, hoping I'm not making a bad decision.

Robert draws his sword and puts it to Joseph's neck. Joseph reaches for his own blade, but I knock his hand away. I take his sword out myself and hold it on him. Robert and I work together to keep Joseph from doing a thing.

"What's going on, Arabella?" Robert asks. His voice is tinted with the faintest bit of worry, but he mostly sounds firm and in control. Abner looks on with concern.

I explain what happened, fear shaking my voice.

Abner curses. "We can't let them hurt her."

I nod. "I have a plan."

Chapter
TWENTY-EIGHT

∽

"Y OU REALLY THINK this will work?" Abner asks.

"I do." I put more conviction than I feel behind the words. If my plan fails, there won't be a second chance. It has to work.

"Then you should let me go," he says.

"No," Robert and I say at the same time.

"I don't know how they feel about hurting you," I say. "Besides, there's enough royalty at risk already with me going back into that room."

"But Robert—" Abner starts.

"Is a safer choice than you," Robert replies.

"We need to get going. I don't know how long they'll wait before they start hurting her."

"I'll round the guards around the castle's entrances, so they can't escape," Abner says and turns to Robert. "Stay safe, my friend."

"I will."

"And you, Arabella." Abner faces me, his voice growing fainter. "I'm sorry for all the trouble I caused. Sorrier now than ever before. I should have never lied to you."

His words soften my heart toward him. Maybe there's more good in him than I gave him credit for. "You are entirely forgiven."

"Stay safe."

I look at my future groom. My heart doesn't warm—not exactly—but it feels at peace. "I will."

"Now what?" Robert says.

"Take a hold of my wrist, like Joseph was doing when we first ran into you." I can't believe I'm telling him to touch me, and in front of my future husband. Still, when he grabs a hold of me, a tingle of warmth rushes up my arm.

I study Joseph's face as Robert continues to hold a sword on him. I can't mess this up; it has to be perfect. When I'm certain I know it all, I cast my spell through my wrist, up Robert's arm, and to his face. I change his features to look like Joseph's. He gives a small hiss of pain, but otherwise all goes well.

"That's creepy," Abner says.

"Thanks," Robert replies.

"You still sound like yourself," I say. "Try to make your voice sound less deep."

"Like this?"

"Better." Though it will still be hard to pass him off as Joseph, I hope it's enough.

"Now we have to be careful not to let Aiden touch me, or the spell will wear off," I say.

Robert smiles. "Keep my voice higher, don't let Aiden touch you, and save Jocelyn. We can do this."

I hope he's right. My doubts grow by the second. What was I thinking? I know—the importance of joining our two races is greater than that of one life. But it's Jocelyn's life. I can't let anything bad happen to her.

"Let's go," I say.

Abner takes over putting a sword to Joseph's throat and watches as we head back the way I came. No doubt the guards will be everywhere as soon as he tells them. I walk slowly, giving him a chance to call the guards and set them in place. No matter what happens, we can't have those three escaping. Not again.

Despite my pace, we reach the room too quickly. I pause at the entrance. Robert gives my wrist a squeeze, and then opens the door.

The room is as I left it, and Aiden moves to put the dagger back at Jocelyn's neck the moment I step inside.

True to instruction, Robert doesn't let go of my wrist. He can't yet, or all will be lost.

"I've done it," I say, putting the fear I feel for Jocelyn's life in my voice. "I told them the marriage was off. For good this time."

Octavian looks to Robert, who appears every bit as Joseph. Robert nods. Smart man, keeping the talking to a minimum.

"It's done." Glee fills Octavian's voice. "I'll finally have my reward."

Confusion muddles my thoughts. "What reward?"

"Don't you worry about it."

"Let's go," Aiden says.

"Wait," I say. "I know I'm no longer in a position to bargain, but please, let Jocelyn go. I promise I'll behave if only you don't make her come with us."

"And have her tell everyone what we've done?" Octavian says. "I don't think so."

"*Please.*"

"Don't get watery," Aiden says. "We're not going to hurt her, as long as you cooperate."

He moves the dagger away from her neck and sheathes it. Inside, I'm cheering for the new development. Outwardly, I sniff like I'm still scared.

Suddenly, Aiden narrows his eyes at Robert's hand around my wrist. "What is—?"

Robert jumps forward. I leap into action, thrusting my sword toward Aiden and making space for Jocelyn to escape. Robert pulls out his own blade and jumps it into the fray. Aiden reaches for me, but I swing my sword toward his hand.

He darts back, grabs Jocelyn as she passes by, and puts the dagger to her throat again.

"You can't win," Octavian says. "We warned you what would happen if you didn't do what we said."

"Don't harm her. If you do, I'll never, ever do what you want."

Aiden and Octavian exchange a look. Robert is heaving close to them. If he reached out, he'd be able to touch them with his sword.

"Come here, then," Octavian says. "Exchange your life for hers. I see Robert knows, which means you probably told others, and our original plan isn't going to work. Give yourself over, and she goes free."

I hesitate. Not because I don't want to save Jocelyn, but because if I go with them, there's no more leverage left.

"Don't do it," Robert says.

I hover between the two. "How do I know you'll let her go?"

"You're going to have to trust us," Aiden says.

"Like I can do that." I whip my sword toward his dagger hand and slice his wrist open. He drops the dagger with a cry. Jocelyn tries to run away, but Octavian grabs her arm and yanks her back. She elbows him, and he smacks her upside the head.

I thrust my sword to the side, but Aiden has recovered and blocks me. This room is too cramped for fighting. Still, I give it my all against Aiden. Our swords fly fast, almost faster than I can keep track of. It's reaction after reaction. I'm more grateful than ever for all the lessons my teacher gave me. Without them, I'd never hold my own against Aiden.

Robert tries to jump in, but there's not enough room. He puts in his sword, but it gets in the way more than it helps because of the space.

Aiden gets past my defenses to slice into my shoulder. I don't cry out, but the pain ratchets through me. At least it wasn't my sword arm.

We fight, the fray growing hotter and more dangerous. My breath comes in sharp gasps, and sweat runs down my forehead. Robert manages to stab at Aiden, but he blocks it. It leaves Aiden open, and I take the opportunity to slash at him.

He drops his sword with a curse. I turn on Octavian, and he lets Jocelyn go.

As soon as she's safe, I back toward the door, relief filling me. Robert follows, our swords pointed at our would-be attackers.

"Run and get help," I tell Jocelyn. "There should be some guards close by."

It doesn't take long for her to return with them, and for the guards to take away our prisoners. I don't know what will happen to them, but I hope the king isn't lenient. As much as I don't wish for death on another, Octavian and Aiden have caused too much trouble to be left to languish around.

Chapter
TWENTY-NINE

L ATE THE NEXT DAY, I'm worn out, but still standing before the human king and queen. I need to find out what fate will befall my attackers before I can get some rest. I forced Jocelyn to lie down, though. I can tell her later what happened to them.

She's probably cleaning or something, instead of resting. I tried.

Everyone is here. The king, the queen, the princess, Abner, and Robert, who stands behind Abner's throne. Octavian and Aiden are nowhere in sight.

"We understand you've had a trying time of it," the king says. "I'm so sorry for all you've gone through while under our protection. Thank you for apprehending the criminals."

"I was just doing what I thought was best," I say. "I'll be grateful when the attacks on my life end."

"I don't know if they ever will." He heaves a sigh that speaks of a lifetime of troubles. "But we should have a better chance for you now. Aiden and Octavian are on lockdown and in a boat back to Amara. We sent word about what happened, along with a note saying we think they both should be executed so this type of thing doesn't happen again."

I nod my agreement, my throat too thick for me to force words past.

"We found the elf who brought you the note. He and Joseph is in our dungeons. We hate to punish him too harshly, as we think he's acting on instinct and not malice, but rest assured, both he and the elf servant who did this to you will be locked up for a very long time."

My heart wrenches at the thought of Joseph's betrayal. All I can do now is hope he changes his mind about me marrying Abner and doesn't have to spend too long in prison. Though, if he's going to act like he did, the prison is probably the best place for him. I don't want him to have to stay there. Not after I became friends with him. It's all so convoluted. It's hard to know exactly what to think and feel.

"The only real threat we have left is the pirates. Captain Smythe is nowhere to be found, but we'll keep looking and keep you and my son well-guarded until such a time as he is found."

"Thank you for your protection," I say.

"I am sorry so much of it is needed. Sorry that I couldn't protect you in my own castle."

Me too.

"You've been very brave and fearless," the queen says.

"Fear has been following me through out this whole thing."

"But your actions say otherwise," she says. "I am sorry your first foray to our country has been one of such hardship. I would not have it so."

"It hasn't all been hard. There have been good things too. I'm grateful to have met your family and become more a part of you before I marry your son."

"And we've been glad to get to know you a little better. Next opportunity for you to come, I promise we'll show you a grand time, a safer one as well. If you decide to go on tour, we'll make certain you have plenty of trustworthy guards."

I don't know if she can follow through on that promise. I thought Joseph was trustworthy. We all did. Look where that got us. Nowhere useful—that's for certain.

"We will be leaving in the morning," she says.

"We'll be ready to go," I reply.

"I will not be joining you on this initial journey," Princess Belle says. "I have some things I need to take care of here, first." Probably more things for her mother.

"I will look forward to seeing you, when you can join us," I say. "I want to show you some of the sights Omanska has to offer."

"I look forward to it as well."

Once I am dismissed, I hurry back to my rooms, careful not to look too closely at Robert before I go. My guards follow at a respectful distance. I don't like having them so close all the time, more for what they represent than for their actual presence.

"What news have you?" Jocelyn asks as soon as I open the door.

I shut it behind me. Might as well get to the heart of what she wants to know so I can be done thinking about it. "Octavian and Aiden are being sent home, with a note that requests their execution."

She puts a hand to her throat. "Oh my."

"Yes—well—as much as I'm against bloodshed, it's probably for the best. We'll see what my parents have to say over the matter."

"I'm sure they'll agree to the safest course of action for you."

"Of course." I just hate to be the cause of someone's death, no matter how much they may deserve it. "Are we all ready to go for tomorrow?"

"We should be good."

"Yes... I hope we're done with being attacked for quite some time." But with pirates still out there, lurking, who knows what will happen? I'll not feel safe until Captain Smythe has been captured.

Chapter
THIRTY

❧

I SIT IN THE CARRIAGE in the courtyard, surrounded by dozens of guards. There's no way a pirate or anyone else will attack with so many of them. Physically, I'm safe, though my heart feels anything but. I don't know what I should be feeling. Happy maybe. I am going to my wedding day, after all. And now know who I'm marrying. Abner's still not one of my favorite people, but I've seen a hint of why he's Robert's best friend. It doesn't mean I want to marry him.

But I will. For the good of both my country and his.

Robert comes out and sits in the carriage behind mine with Jocelyn. Having them at my back is comforting, though I wish we were going in the same carriage.

Abner comes out next. He's dressed in his finest, looking more like Prince Phillip than ever before. It doesn't help that we're matching, but it's what's needed—the two of us showing a united front.

No matter what we show, there's still tension in the air. Still a threat lingering. It's evident in the guards placed strategically around us. In the way the crowd is silently watching us from the gates. I'm surprised they aren't cheering for their prince. Maybe it's different here, though. Maybe how they show respect is with their silence.

Yet, I can't help but feel it's more. That there's something hovering in the crowd.

Abner gets in the carriage and sits down next to me. Being so close makes me nervous. There's nowhere to go. No scooting over to get some distance. As I look at the calm expression on his face, I think maybe he will help me do what's needed for our countries, even if neither of us wants this.

I tell him, "I think I'm ready to be married."

He turns to me, brows lifted. "You are? I didn't think that would ever happen. Or if it did, it wouldn't be for years."

"Yes, I am. I think you've earned it. I'm just sorry it had to be this way instead of what we both desire."

He glances at the carriage behind us. At first I think he's looking at Robert and thinking of me, but a wistful tone enters his voice that makes me wonder. "I think we both deserve more. Deserve what we wish for. But I also know we're strong enough to put our own wants to the side."

I follow his gaze, not to Robert, but to Jocelyn. "Do you—?" I shake my head. Even if he does, it doesn't matter. "Never mind."

The king and queen come out then, and the king helps his wife into the carriage ahead of ours. This is it—the last journey before I wed Abner and join our two nations. I'm anxious for the crossing. I've seen too much pain and heartache and turmoil going on between our two races to allow it to continue. I need to wed him.

The carriages pull forward, the guards marching with us as we go. We exit the courtyard, and the people waiting on the sides of the street are silent. Eerily so. I can't decide if it's good or not. They aren't screaming against us or throwing things, but it feels like they'd like to.

How can I stop this? How can I help them see that human or elf—it doesn't matter? We are the same, even if there are differences between us. Magic isn't something to be afraid of, especially since it's waning. And technology isn't something to be scared of either. They need to understand this, but I don't know how to show them.

Then I think about what I'm doing. How I'm acting. I'm sitting stiff, leaning as far away from Abner as I can manage. No wonder the people are glaring at me. I'm rejecting their prince. Time to change that, even if it's the last thing I want to do.

I shift my position so I'm close to Abner, almost leaning into him. He lifts his brows at me.

"If we want the people to unite, we need to be united ourselves," I say.

"Very well." He slips an arm around me, and the crowd gasps.

I stiffen a moment, unused to the contact from a man, but then I relax into him. Those gathered around us are sporting different looks. Some I can make out, some I can't. Those I see are anything from shocked to angry and from happy to confused. I'm right there with them. I don't know how to feel about this latest development.

What I do want is to look behind me. To see what Robert thinks of Abner's arm around me, and of me leaning into him. But I can't glance behind me. I can't see what the man I desire to have his arm around me thinks of another man putting doing so.

As the crowds pass by, they grow more emotional.

Their eyes watch us, taking in our position together.

I'd like to think we're making a difference, but some of the scowls directed at me make me believe otherwise.

Someone shouts, "Down with the elf."

Abner holds me closer, putting his hand over mine where it rests on my lap. Accepting me, even if his people haven't yet. Will there be repercussions because of this? Will his people reject him if he receives me?

We're almost to the docks now. I can see them up ahead, far past the guards leading us. I have to make it there, and then everything will be back to normal. At least until we reach Amara.

Though normal is relative, it has to be better than these sidelong glances and glares. Better than the whispers and hateful words. I've been shielded by the hate by being among the people in disguise. But now it's out. The people aren't going to stand for me with their prince.

I remind myself that he doesn't agree with them. The way he clasps my hand, I know his support is greater than the glare of the human race.

Out of the corner of my eye, I see someone stand up on a rock. The height catches my attention. Though the crowd is borderline hostile, I hope whoever is getting up wants a better look at their prince and future princess. I glance over at him as they release an arrow. An arrow headed straight for me.

Time slows. I'm frozen, mouth gaping, ready to scream, but nothing comes out. The arrow nears. My heart pounds. I'm not going to live. After all this, I'm to be killed before I reach home. Before I see my parents. Before I unite our two countries.

What will my people think? What will happen when the elves find out I've been murdered by a human? The world will go in disarray.

The arrow nears. It's going to hit. Abner shifts in front of me. Time speeds up. Abner's on the floor of the carriage, an arrow through his chest.

"*No*," I scream.

The world around me becomes a noisy blur. I kneel down next to Abner.

Should I take the arrow out? Leave it in? Put pressure around the wound? I don't know, and he's growing grayer by the second. I don't know exactly what to do about the wound, but I do know how to heal with magic. I grab his hand and send health his way.

Our carriage stops, and Robert's there, the king and some guards close behind. The crowd is noisy, but giving us space.

Abner grips Robert's hand, tight. "Promise me you'll marry Arabella."

Robert glances up at me. I try not to focus on it, but only on healing Abner. Making him better. The magic isn't doing much good, though. I don't know how to make this better.

"Promise me." Abner strains, surprising me with how hard he's trying to get these last words out.

"I promise," Robert responds, voice tight.

My heart sinks, not because of the words, but because Abner is dying. Dying because of me.

"Tell Jocelyn… I love her." Abner's last words are faint. His face goes lifeless.

I glance up to find Jocelyn in the carriage behind us, pale. Who is going to tell her?

Abner's father is calling out orders to the guards. Abner's mother is fighting to get to us while guards are trying to move her back toward the castle. Men are moving everywhere. The crowd is a discordant array of noise. Everything around us is chaos. I'm sobbing without realizing when I started.

Everything we worked for, bringing humans and elves together, is going to be undone by one moment. A moment that should have ended my life.

But instead, the human prince lies at my side, dead.

Chapter
THIRTY-ONE

～

THE SOUND OF A MOURNFUL horn echoes through the valley. The only sound for miles. Except for the tears of mourners. I don't feel right, mourning Abner; it's somehow a betrayal of all my feelings from before. But I do mourn him.

I forgave him after all. We were making amends as best we could. We were about to be married, and I'm certain we could have made it work somehow.

Instead, he gave his life for mine.

It's a rude awakening of how much violence people are capable of. I saw it in the pirates, but when they found the person responsible for the murder, it wasn't a pirate. It was an average human citizen. One who was distraught over killing the wrong person.

And now he's gone as well. The king was swift in his judgment for the murderer of his only son. Death by hanging. It was done in public, big and drawn out, like a warning for others who would try. Would it have been the same if I was the one killed?

It doesn't matter. I'm still here, full of guilt but not as much sorrow as Jocelyn. I wrap my arm around my best friend as she sobs. I had no idea she cared so deeply about the man I was supposed to marry. I would have been far happier if he was still alive and could marry her instead. I don't know if Robert has told her Abner's final words.

I haven't spoken to Robert at all.

It doesn't matter what Abner was asked of Robert; it can't come to pass. Now that the heir to the throne is Abner's sister, I don't know what's to become of me. At least, I assume she's the heir. She's the next oldest child, the only other child. It has to be her, though she doesn't seem to want it.

Robert is still just Robert. I can't imagine my parents ever agreeing to me marrying someone beneath me. Part of the reason they agreed to the match with Abner in the first place was because he was a prince.

I sigh, trying to let it all go. There are too many thoughts and anxieties to dwell on when I should be in mourning. It's not like I can help it, though. I have my country to worry over, and I honestly am concerned over Bardus as well. What will become of our countries now? I can't do as much as I could when I was going to marry the future leader of Bardus. I only have power over my own country, and that power is diminishing. If I can't make a good match, what can I do?

The horn stops playing. Jocelyn's cries feel me with guilt. Though I know it's not my fault, that guilt doesn't go away.

Even now, we're surrounded by guards, the rest of the mourners half a mile away. Still, I fear someone else could do damage. I'm more prepared for it now, ready to strike with magic, should the need arise, though, I don't know what I could have done to stop an arrow with so little warning.

Which is why I shouldn't feel guilty.

But I do.

Jocelyn's sobs slow. Abner's sister has silent tears running down her face, but the king and queen are stoic. Robert is as well, when I dare glance at him.

The ceremony is over, but no one moves. No one wants to. All our hopes are lost. All we've worked for is gone. All I've suffered was for nothing.

BACK IN THE THRONE ROOM, everyone is weary. I can feel it weaving itself through me and matching the lines and dark circles under the eyes of the others. Jocelyn isn't here. I insisted she take some time for herself. She's done a lot of that lately, but it doesn't feel nearly enough. I wish there was more I could do for her, but I don't know what, besides giving her time and being there for her when she needs me.

The king and queen are both in their thrones, their daughter to one side all wearing the deep purple color humans associate with mourning. The other side, where Abner's chair is, stays empty. Heart-wrenchingly so. Robert stands behind it, where I've seen him before.

And I stand alone, in front of them all also wearing deep purple in honor of the fallen human prince. If I was at home it'd be a sky blue like the elves wear. Though it's been like this before, it's wasn't nearly as apparent as it is now. Never have I felt so far from what I want and so close to ruining everything.

Forget close. Everything is ruined.

"Thank you all for coming," the king says. His voice is strained, like speaking is a trial for him. "I hate to move on so quickly, but there are not just one, but two kingdoms to worry about."

"I'm so sorry for your loss. Abner was a good man." Something I was just beginning to realize. It dawns on me then— I'm the only real representative here for Omanska. I have to do what's best for my country, going forward. I always do, but now it's more imperative than ever.

"We all know Abner's last request." The king looks pointedly at me, and I work hard not to look at Robert. It doesn't matter how much I want to honor Abner's will, I can't imagine ever being able to marry Robert.

"I've spent many hours considering what to do, and I think my final decision is what is best for everyone, but it will mean sacrifices," he says. "Princess Belle, you were to inherit the throne after your brother. Robert, you were next in line after that."

Robert was third and is now second in line for the throne? I had no idea. Why didn't anyone tell me?

"Princess Belle is to take over but has told me there is something she would like to discuss about the matter."

"Yes, there is." She takes a deep breath, seemingly steadying herself. Though it's just me, Robert, and her parents, I hope she can find the right words. I know it'll mean a lot to her in this moment to speak what's in her heart.

"I know that, with time, being heir to the throne is something I could do," she says. "Mom, Dad, you have raised me well. You have given me a better training than one could hope. I appreciate all you have done for me, but being heir was a role well-suited to Phillip. It's not one suited to me. I cannot help but feel stifled by it.

"Not only that, but I think my country would benefit more from the rule cousin Robert can give them. I trust that I could do all right, but he will be a great ruler. I know what my limits are. I abdicate my role as heir to the throne of Bardus."

I hold in a gasp. I can't believe she'd give it up. She is so sweet and could lead the country in a good direction. Despite my feelings, it's not my place to say anything, especially now that we're only friends and not almost sisters. If we weren't in front of the king and queen, I would speak up, but her parents have a right to do it before I do. And cousin? I didn't know Abner and Robert were related. It makes sense now that I think about it though.

I glance up at them. They have such serene expressions. Belle must have spoken to them about this before she made the decision.

This makes me feel a little better, but she's still giving up so much.

It's Robert who speaks up. "Are you certain, Belle? I know you could do great things."

"It's true. I probably could. But I believe someone like you could do better. This is the best thing I can do for my country and my people. I will still act as princess, but not heir to the throne. That is yours, should you choose to accept it."

Robert moves to Belle and says something too quietly for me to hear. Then he kneels before the king, queen, and Princess Belle. "I accept being heir to the throne and promise to treat it with the respect and dignity the position commands."

"Very well," the king says. "You may rise."

"We talked long about this possibility," says the queen. "We knew that, while you are not our sweet Abner, you would be a good fit to the throne. We are grateful you accept this responsibility."

"As the heir to the throne," the king says, "you are free not only to fulfill Abner's wishes, but to marry the elven Princess Arabella, and thus unite our nation and hers."

My heart floats away. Did he really say what I think he did? My feet feel cemented to the floor. I can't imagine this being real. It has to be a dream. It just has to.

Robert's face is what convinces me it's real. He's as shocked as I am.

After just a short second, he rushes to me and gets down on one knee. "Arabella?"

"Yes," is all I can manage.

"Will you marry me?"

Technically, I shouldn't say anything without my parents' permission, but they have to understand. Our two countries need this to happen now. My parents need to know we're serious about uniting our people. Besides, though this is Robert instead of Abner, he holds the same position Abner did.

And more than anything else, I want to marry him.

"Yes. I will," I say, keeping the happiness I feel over marrying the man I love subdued so it doesn't overshadow the loss everyone is dealing with. "I will."

He takes both my hands in his and stands. "We should marry soon."

"The sooner the better," the king says. "You two, along with any who will attend the wedding, must leave at once for Amara."

"I promise to make you proud and to make sure Abner would approve of mine and Robert's actions."

The queen gives a nod. "Thank you."

This is it, then. Who knew when things started out the way they did with my wedding to Abner that I would end up here? I can't help but feel like I've been given a chance I need to grab a hold of. Nothing can stop me this time. Not even pirates. I will do this.

As Robert leads me out, I know we will make a wonderful team, uniting two nations as they should be. Under us, they'll find peace and harmony. It may take time, but I know we can do it.

And that's not the best part. Nothing can overshadow the fact that I'm getting married to the man I love.

about the
AUTHOR
◦∾◦

AMAZON BEST SELLING author Janeal Falor lives in Utah with her husband and three children. In her non-writing time she teaches her kids to make silly faces, cooks whatever strikes her fancy, and attempts to cultivate a garden even when half the things she plants die. When it's time for a break she can be found taking a scenic drive with her family, fencing, or drinking hot chocolate.

SIGN UP TO RECEIVE RELEASE NOTIFICATIONS AT:

www.janealfalor.com

ACKNOWLEDGEMENTS

EVERY BOOK I MAKE is a collection of not just my world and thoughts, but comes together with the help of so many other people. Everyone of them is special to me and I appreciate all their help. Any faults left are all my own, but I know there would be many more had they not helped.

Thank you to my beta readers. Wil Scott for looking over my series. Tracey Joesph for helping me expand and explore my word. Marie Krepps for finding holes and giving praise when I needed it.

Huge thanks to Karen C. Eddington, without whom this book would be a deary thought in my head instead of an entire book.

Thank you to Sotia Lazu for copy editing and making me laugh. Also, thank you to Yeseina Vargas for polishing up my work so it reads cleanly.

My family deserves my thanks as well. They are always there for me, supporting my hobby. They encourage me, praise me, and cheer me on. I would never be able to write without their support.

Dear reader, thank you for joining me on Arabella's journey. I love hearing from you and enjoy your comments on my stories. You guys make my day! Thank you!

www.ingramcontent.com/pod-product-compliance
Lightning Source LLC
Chambersburg PA
CBHW060641260626
47161CB00008B/2943